TENDER LOVING CARE: STORIES OF A WEST VIRGINIA DOCTOR VOLUME TWO

Stories of Harold Almond, MD
as told to
Greenbrier Almond, MD

Greenbrier Almond MD

(2011)

International Standard Book Number 0-87012-728-4
Library of Congress Control Number 2005900418
Printed in the United States of America
Copyright © 2005 by Dr. Greenbrier Almond
Buckhannon, West Virginia
All Rights Reserved
2011

Printed
2005
2006
2011

Printed by
McClain Printing Company
Parsons, WV
www.mcclainprinting.com
2011

Cover photo by Lois Flanagan Almond.

Illustrations courtesy of
**The Upshur County
Historical Society**

Originally printed in the
Buckhannon Record.

DEDICATION

Dedicated to the loving memory of my best friend, my wife, Lois. And to our children—Greenbrier, K, Anne, Ruthie, and Beth—who added joy and pride to our lives. And to all my collies, who faithfully loved their master as he loved them.

-Harold Almond, MD
Dedication from
The Stories of a West Virginia Doctor
6/1/1997

Following my injuries of July 3, 2004, my loving wife Araceli cared for me and encouraged me in the writing of this second volume of stories. Our children Maria and Ronce wanted more of their granddad's stories recorded. So these are dedicated to them and to the other grandchildren of Harold and Lois Almond including Taylor, Joseph, Chris, Jesse, and Ginger, and the newest addition to the family, a great-granddaughter Caroline Georgia.

-Greenbrier Almond, MD
11/01/2004

ACKNOWLEDGEMENTS

A special thanks to my children for their enthusiasm and help. To my doctor son, Greenbrier, for always asking questions and carefully listening to my stories. To my oldest daughter, K, for her frequent visits to look after daily details and for our hours of good talks. To my daughter, Anne, for her organizational talent as she undertook the task of editor for my book. To my daughter, Ruthie, for her numerous letters and calls of support. To my daughter, Beth, for her writing contributions and her eagle-eye proofreading. To my son-in-law, Richard, for using his computer expertise to format my book. I also wish to thank my friend, Judy Knorr, for her word-processing and proofreading assistance. I especially wish to thank my medical colleagues, my nursing staff, and my patients, who blessed me with a long and satisfying practice.

-Harold Almond, MD
Acknowledgments from
The Stories of a West Virginia Doctor
6/1/1997

Additional thanks for this second volume of stories goes to channel 3, the local access TV station in Buckhannon which has aired the Tender Loving Care program weekly for twenty-six years. Also, thanks to Kimberly Link Gilmore who has great editing skills. Her intelligent questioning led to significant improvements in the stories.

-Greenbrier Almond, MD
11/01/2004

TABLE OF CONTENTS

PREFACE

The title of this book, *Tender Loving Care: Stories of a West Virginia Doctor*, was inspired by the appearances of Dr. Harold D. Almond on the weekly television program I've hosted on the local access channel in Buckhannon, West Virginia for the last twenty-six years. Dad appeared fifty-two times as a special guest on the show.

That he was well loved by the community is an understatement. Once an old veteran patient from Ellamore, a rural community on the banks of the Middle Fork of the Tygart River, presented for examination and treatment in my Veteran's Administration clinic. He greeted me as I entered the exam room with a salute. He said, "Doc, I tune into your program every week." That was music to my ears. I thanked him profusely. Then he added, "Yes, Doc, I tune in every week and if your Dad is your guest, then I leave the TV on and watch the show."

Dad's first book, *The Stories of a West Virginia Doctor*, has been a remarkable "best seller" for McClain Printing in Parsons, West Virginia. Even now "Stories" retails in more than fifty bookstores and gift shops throughout West Virginia. The reception was most gratifying to Dad in 1997 when the West Virginia University Medical School Dean and Associate Dean praised Dad. Upon reading the book, Associate Dean D.Z. Morgan wrote to Harold, "You have had a more colorful life than I have!" The Dean of the Medical School, Robert D'Alessandri, bought copies of Doc's book for all the medical students and for all faculty. He invited Doc to come on the opening day of school and tell three of his stories as part of the opening assembly. The Dean graciously told his students and faculty that "Dr. Harold D. Almond is a sterling example of primary care." The Dean further said, "In medicine,

1

heritage and continuity with the past is important. Dr. Harold Almond is among the few doctors who have written down their stories. You will learn much about the scientific basis of medicine in the next four years, but today you will learn much about the compassion and caring of our healing profession." Dr. Harold Almond held court at an autograph table where students chatted informally and had their personal copies signed by this esteemed physician. The tradition of a colorful life devoted to the practice of medicine continued.

So many blessings have come my way from Dad taking the extra time and effort to publish some of his stories. For example, while making hospital rounds with students at the Veteran's Administration Hospital I commented to one red-headed lass that she had the same last name as one of my favorite local pastors in Upshur County. She beamed and said that was her grandfather.

My interest piqued, I asked her if she knew of Dad's book. "Yes indeed," she replied. "That's my family's story on page 25." I recalled the story of the little baby girl born to deaf parents and the excitement of her four-year-old big brother when the newborn cried out, meaning she would be able to speak. I remembered how Dad loved this family and my heart thrilled.

The writing of the first book proved natural for Dad. His sister Grace characterized her brother well when she told family and friends at the 50th wedding anniversary celebration for Harold and Lois, "My brother was born with a library card in his mouth!"

The culmination of an abundant life of reading Perry Mason mysteries, medical and surgical texts, every book written about General Douglas MacArthur, West Virginia histories, and most anything else, was found in his

2

authoring of *The Stories of a West Virginia Doctor*. Doc said on the Tender Loving Care TV program, "When I was too old to practice medicine, too old to weed strawberries, and too old to pick strawberries, it was time to write my memoirs." He admitted that he left out many stories in anticipation of another book.

For five years since Dad's death I've prayed for an opportunity to write more of the stories Dad wished to tell. On July 3rd, 2004 in a freak accident I fractured my pelvis and was rendered immobile for six weeks. The pain proved severe but I thank God he gave me a physician wife, Araceli, who cared for me. And for a double blessing, our daughter, Maria, was able to stay home from Harvard Medical School for a month to help too. Our son, Ronce, in the midst of working with a Presidential political campaign also came home frequently. He had our house remote computer ready for a laptop I could manage and a bed placed in view of the television. Now I was ready to watch and analyze all fifty-two video tapes of Dad's guest spots on the Tender Loving Care TV program. From that, I wrote seventy additional stories for the new book.

Dr. Patrick Galey, my orthopedic surgeon, told me I was to learn patience from this pelvic fracture experience. Yes, I agree. And more! My desire is that these stories will convey my rediscovery of hope from my pioneering, trail-blazing Dad. Please pay attention to the steady, constant calling of a warm, personal God-fearing physician, conveyed especially in the stories, "I am Willing" and "Most Chosen." Please note the love of family, patients, community, country and God.

-Dr. Greenbrier Almond, 11/01/2004

HOUSE CALLS

4-H CAMP CALL

Greenbrier remembers:

"Let's go, Greenbrier," Dad said as he kissed my Mom goodbye, adding, "I'll take good care of him, Sugar Plum."

Brier, our collie dog, and I were definitely excited. He wagged his tail and I rubbed his ears really hard just as he liked. We both shared shotgun in the green Jeep Dad used for house calls. Our destination was the Upshur County Youth Camp in Selbyville where Dad would perform screening physical exams on 4-H campers, ensuring that no infectious diseases would disrupt camp. I was only five years old, but already I'd heard of polio. Mom always said, "Little pitchers have big ears," meaning I heard everything the grown-ups talked about around the kitchen table.

The camp nurse had set up our office on the McDade House porch. The Cherokee, Delaware, Mingo, and Seneca Tribes lined up out on the green lawn awaiting their turn. Dad looked out over the expansive bottom making up the camp grounds. Then he asked the Big Foot Chief to have the 4-H'ers give a big "HOW HOW" cheer, so loud that there would be an echo off the surrounding mountains. Brier and I were impressed.

One by one the campers came by. Each said "ahhh" as Dad applied a tongue depressor while he studied their throats. I watched as he checked for lymph nodes, listened to the hearts and lungs, and examined hands and skin for sores. All the while Dad inquired of each child which 4-H project he had completed prior to coming to camp. He particularly praised campers who had brought farm produce with them as payment for camp fees.

All campers were present and accounted for, and all were healthy.

Heading down the road I longed for the day I would be old enough for 4-H camp. Dad said I was growing up just like Jesus, thanks to Mom. He recited Luke 2:52, the 4-H Bible verse: "And Jesus increased in wisdom and stature, and in favor with God and man."

#10 on F. B. I. TOP 10 LIST

In Doc's senior year of medical school he had studied tropical medicine. Later when he served in Japan in the post-WW II occupation he looked out for Dengue Fever, the most common mosquito-borne virus, but never saw a case. The severe pain associated with generalized muscle aches, headache, retro-orbital pressure, photophobia, backache, and severe malaise intrigued Doc. The rash that resembles measles with its initial flush and then erythematous eruption on face, neck, and chest added to the puzzle. The high fever followed by chills, altered taste sensation, anorexia, nausea, abdominal tenderness, sore throat, vomiting, and depression made the syndrome #10 on Doc's Top 10 Most Wanted F.B.I. List, his running list of diseases for which he was always on the lookout.

Doc left Japan and Asia still looking.

Then one cold January night he got a call for urgent care at Cleveland, West Virginia. Doc knew he had an unknown diagnosis and a mystery to solve. He braved the inclement weather eagerly. Reaching the county line, he turned left after entering Webster County at the bridge and drove another half-mile up a snow drifted country road. A sergeant who had just returned from Southeast Asia two weeks earlier was bent over with pain. He had erythematous eruption over his face, neck, and trunk. His temperature was 104 degrees Fahrenheit. Doc was thrilled to be able to help. In his gut he knew this syndrome was Dengue Fever. He drew blood to confirm his suspicion. Upon returning home he mailed the specimen to the Charleston State Health Department and they in turn forwarded it on to the Center for Disease Control in Atlanta.

The laboratory report was wired back: "Tell your physician he has diagnosed the first case of Dengue Fever ever found in West Virginia. And be sure to kill all the mosquitoes promptly!"

Doc laughed. His patient would fight off the infection successfully. Old man winter lowered the temperature to zero so no mosquitoes would survive to spread the infection. Mission accomplished.

FATHER AND SON HOUSE CALL

When ten-year-old Greenbrier's best friend died in a tragic farm accident in the summer of 1958, Doc wanted to talk "man to man." The two set out on a long house call to Hemlock, West Virginia, stopping for gas and Popsicles at Craven's Store in Tallmansville.

The hay smelled sweet as it lay in the mown fields. Rickey had been making hay with his grandfather when the accident occurred. The medical details of his concussion and closed head injury dominated their conversation as the old Jeep wound its way up the road.

Climbing up out of Queens, its broad valley eroded throughout eons of time by the Middle Fork of the Tygart River, father and son talked of the father's Boy Scout camping days in New Jersey. As fourth grade ended at Academy School, Rickey and Greenbrier had pledged to one another that they'd camp together on the Summer's Brushy Fork farm—the same farm where the accident would later happen.

Now in "God's Country" high on Hemlock Ridge, the father and son on their house call mission, they turned down a country lane into deep woods. The Braines were the oldest couple in this isolated rural mountain community. Neighbors took turns checking on them and bringing in supplies. The farm had been the birthplace of Mitilda, now in her eighties.

Recent thunderstorms had knocked down several trees. Doc was prepared with axe and saw; with great effort father and son cut their way through. Doc then had to switch into four-wheel drive to navigate the washed-out road the final quarter of a mile. Entering a clearing, the duo was amazed. Cows, goats, chickens and pigs moved lazily around a central two-story log home. A split rail fence protected the orchard on the hillside, and the garden grew to the side without a weed.

Doc exclaimed with delight, "This is the most beautiful farm in the county!" Just then the Braine's door opened and father and son entered, leaving the bright sunshine for a dark front room with a sick bed set by a massive fireplace at the cabin's end. After careful examination and a shot of penicillin for pneumonia, Doc accepted a cup of coffee for himself and a glass of lemonade for his son.

"Walk down to the waterfall, Doc," old Mr. Braine advised. "Just being there is good for what ails you!"

As father and son stood side by side taking in the natural beauty of the falls, Greenbrier turned to his Dad and requested, "Dad, if I join Boy Scouts, will you take me camping up here at Hemlock?"

GOLD CORE

The old lady had taken to bed and was doing poorly. "Could Doc come up?"

"Yes, I'll be there after lunch."

After leaving the paved road toward Queens, Doc then made a sharp right up the hill and seventy-five yards along the edge of a rock cliff until he came to a slab house.

His patient was on the couch in the front room, her "rheumatism" acting up. Doc prescribed some medication and gave her a shot for the pain. Back on the porch he saw the daughter cracking nuts using a large piece of cylindrical rock about 4 inches in diameter by 12 inches in length.

"Could I have some nuts to take with me? My daughters have 4-H cooking projects and make the best walnut fudge."

"Sure, Doc."

"And what is that you are cracking with?"

"Oh, that's core drilling from the gold mine!"

Indeed, Doc had heard about the Native Americans at Ash Camp digging for gold. "Is it true?"

"Here, take one of the cores," the daughter offered.

Later, Doc sent them away to be analyzed at Northwestern University. The report promptly came back:

"One cent worth of gold."

HOUSE CALLS

How can a doctor drive thirty-six miles one way to a small haven in the hardwoods, make a house call, and then drive home? It simply doesn't make sense. There is neither efficiency nor cost effectiveness built into that equation.

Dr. Harold Almond explained his house calls to Pickens by crediting one remarkable human being, Nell Bennett. Since arriving in Pickens from Ireland in her twenties, she had been the heart and soul of the small mountain community. "She's the post mistress, the telephone operator, the mayor, the nurse, the church youth leader, the weather surveyor, and the town gossip."

Doc related, "Whenever Nell called for a house call she told me what to bring in my doctor bag, whether to have chains ready for the Jeep, and what to expect. Since she was calling on a party line, everyone else also knew the doctor was coming. I could expect to have folks out by their mail boxes waving me down from Czar, Helvetia, High Germany, Skelt, Pickens and clear to Hacker Valley." Ah, the life of a country doctor.

IMPERIAL

Doc knew every country lane and every byway in and around Upshur County. He maintained a reputation as a doctor who would make house calls. This time he and his beloved collie, Brier, were hoofing it; there were no roads into Imperial.

When glass-making was a big industry in West Virginia, white sand was at a premium. Imperial had the whitest sand of all. The best way to reach the destination of Imperial was by train. At its peak, 88 men dug sand and loaded a large train car every day that parked at a special siding. The Pickens B & O train would then come to pick up the load of sand.

Besides a post office, a store, and a rooming house, Imperial had quite a farming community surrounding it. After the train delivered the mail, hundreds of folks would stream in from all directions. If they were across the Buckhannon River, there was a swinging bridge to cross.

Doc and Brier walked two miles over the hill from Indian Camp to treat a sick child from the last remaining family in Imperial. Fortunately, the trail was well trod as eight kids trooped out daily to the bus shed at the end of the school bus run. Quite often after dark they hiked back home on the same trail.

Did Doc expect to be paid for his effort that day? Maybe, maybe not. But as he sat on the front porch after treating the sick child, a family member remembered his profound remark: "You all are richly blessed. This is a most peaceful place!"

INTEGRAL PART

Syndromes fascinated Doc. Rather than one system being diseased, there are multiple systems and organs involved. He enjoyed the challenge of treating a patient with Felty's Syndrome since the interplay of arthritis, blood, and liver disease required solving a clinical mystery. For five years he treated an invalid patient with this particular syndrome.

One cold day he drove the seven miles to her residence to make a house call, as she required a shot of cortisone. Her husband appeared more distraught than she was that day. He explained that the eighty yards of water line from the house to his butcher shop was frozen. The pipe would need to be dug up and that would be quite a job.

Doc, seeing this "epidemic" of frozen pipes all over the county, suggested applying direct current through the pipe. He knew an electrician who had had good results. Diagnosis made. Treatment given. The lady's joints were unfrozen and the pipes were unfrozen, too. All in a day's work.

MOM'S HOME COOKING

The annual Pickens Maple Syrup Festival, always the third weekend in March, grew from word of mouth; people were drawn to this Brigadoon place. Dr. Harold Almond loved the chance to tell stories of Dr. Cunningham and hear stories from the Pickens physician's former patients as they streamed through the Roberts-Cunningham Museum. On this day more than 450 folks stopped by.

The next in line to greet Doc Almond was a middle-aged woman dressed rather shabbily but warmly. She appeared anxious to say something. Even as she began to speak her lip quivered with emotion and her voice broke. She told Doc that he had been her family's physician for forty years. Her foster father had died a while back and her foster mother had just passed on after an extended illness. She wished that he had not retired as she felt her mother would have received good care from him. He had always taken good care of them, especially the time he came to their home saving her life when she was a child of four.

Did he recall her and her family?

They talked on. Her parents, who worked as tenant farmers, took her in though they had little themselves. In fact the day of the well-remembered house call, the road was not passable due to the spring mud. Doc had walked in late at night. After examining the child he had told the parents she was quite ill, but if he gave her a shot of penicillin her fever might break and her double pneumonia might improve. Since it was late and since the little girl was so sick, Doc declared he'd stay the night, catching some shuteye in the rocking chair by the fire.

"Yes," Doc declared, "in the morning you were already getting better. For breakfast, your mother made the best biscuits I've ever eaten."

"Oh, you do remember!" the woman smiled through her tears and hugged Doc.

SAVED BY A SIREN

A call from Rock Cave, as far as the telephone line ran, reported a 12-year old boy gravely ill at Gaines. "Doc, come quickly!" a desperate voice implored.

When Doc arrived at the country lane he pulled up to the first gate, opening it carefully and closing it behind. Then he drove across the pasture to another gate. This too he opened and closed behind. Finally after twelve gates he arrived at the house.

Indeed, the boy had acute meningitis. Getting him back to the hospital for a spinal tap and IV antibiotic would be all that could save his life. But first Doc had to drive back to Rock Cave through those twelve gates and call to town for the funeral home who supplied ambulance service via their hearse.

Promptly, Mr. Conard of Poling St. Clair Funeral Home arrived, and Doc headed back to Gaines from Rock Cave with him. Urgently up through the twelve gates the ambulance drove, this time leaving the gates open after closing the first one. My, how hot the sun beat down. Doc was sweating also because his patient's condition continued to deteriorate. At last, the boy was loaded in the hearse dubbing as an ambulance, and back through the fields Mr. Conard drove.

As they approached the final gate they spied a mountaineer up on a large boulder above the gate. He was taking aim on the ambulance. Doc paused but a second. "Blow your siren," he yelled, "he's going to shoot us!"

The siren's shrill blaring split the heat!

Startled, the marksman mountain man dropped his gun and bound away. The ambulance sped through the gate and off to St. Joseph's Hospital. The young patient survived along with his physician and ambulance crew—saved by a siren.

SECOND CHANCE

Doc did not pretend to be a theologian when he told his stories to the TLC TV program viewing audience. He did, however, understand life and death. With a turn of a phrase he pointed his patients in the right direction.

Raising the dead to life based on Dr. Luke's account of Jesus raising Lazarus from the dead made for a weighty Easter season topic. Doc had performed a cesarean section on a dead woman who was pregnant with child, saving the life of the little girl.

Reaching back in his vast repertoire of stories, Doc told another amazing story. He had been at home with his family one evening when the phone rang. "Doc, my husband is dying. Can you come quick?" pleaded the lady on the line. She gave directions and Doc left immediately. He knew the house just down on East Main Street.

He arrived within minutes of the call. The patient appeared ashen and clammy. He breathed his last breath. Doc began CPR. Just as a physician hopes, the patient revived.

The gentleman described his near-death experience. He found himself descending circular stairs down, down, down. The temperature was getting hotter and hotter. There was the smell of sulfur.

As the ambulance arrived to take the patient to the hospital, Doc simply said, "Not everyone gets a second chance to change their ways!"

TEST DRIVE

"Ole Friendly" wanted Doc to test drive one of the new Dodge four-wheel drive vans. Ole Friendly's Chrysler-Dodge-Plymouth dealership wanted Doc's business. It was general knowledge that Doc paid cash for his Jeeps. This probably was a throwback to the Great Depression. Anyway, "Ole Friendly" was a persistent salesman. He knew the weakness of the Willys Jeep with its lame clutch and the poor quality heater. "Doc, just call me anytime and we'll go on one of your country calls together."

"Ole Friendly" Bud Bennett served as fire chief for the Buckhannon Fire Department and was as dedicated to community service as Doc. There was a mutual admiration one for the other. However, Doc remained fiercely loyal to his signature green Jeep.

Needless to say there was some high excitement in the Almond home when over the supper table Doc announced he had a house call to make thirty miles up the Buckhannon River to Newlon and he was planning to test drive a new Dodge. Greenbrier, his ten-year old son, wanted to come and since school was out due to excessive snow, Doc's wife, Lois, said okay. Charlie Beer, Doc's sidekick on many night calls would be along too. He was a sounding board for Doc's ideas. Certainly he knew automobiles and trucks as an insurance adjuster.

House calls often began when the evening office closed. Doc stayed open until 9:00 pm Mondays, Wednesdays, and Fridays. This night the snow blowing and the near zero temperature kept most patients home. The nurse could go home early and stoke her fires, Doc offered.

What a huge Dodge Van "Ole Friendly" drove up the hill to the Almond residence! It was fire engine red and thrilled the five children who climbed all over the three rows of seats. After inspection and a goodbye kiss between Doc and Lois, the house call team was off.

Indeed, the blizzard of 1958 raged as the team approached the French Creek Game Farm. Oh my, those poor animals, Greenbrier shivered. The State Road Commission met the Dodge at the turn-off at Routes 4 and 20 South to plow ahead toward Selbyville and then on to Newlon. The artic cold wind had drifted the snow, closing the road. The team pressed on, a giant snow plow followed by the red Dodge.

All night long at a snail's pace Charlie drove. "Ole Friendly" offered Sasperillo to young Greenbrier who was shy to accept. Doc got some shuteye. As dawn broke over Brooks Hill, the crew made their way to a home where a little girl suffered with headache, stiff neck, high fever and increasing stupor. Doc determined it was probable meningitis and she must be hospitalized. So now the big red Dodge really came in handy. The young patient stretched out on the big third seat of the van as it followed the snow plow back across the mountains.

What a test drive, with "Ole Friendly" proud of the way the van had handled the precarious trip. Even so, Doc kept his beloved Jeep!

THANKSGIVING TO EASTER

Doc surprised his faithful TV viewers when he recalled a season of house calls by noting he did not sleep all night in his own bed from Thanksgiving to Easter. One patient called in to say he knew Doc to be 100% available. Others wondered how he could do it.

Doc further noted that he developed an ability to "sleep whenever I could." He said the couch in the doctors' lounge at St. Joseph's Hospital provided an excellent sleep. Greenbrier recalled as a little boy going to medical meetings with his father. Whenever the meeting room lights went down and the slides turned on, his father would be fast asleep.

Grateful patients probably did not know the sacrifice entailed in those all-night house calls, not to mention the years of nighttime deliveries. Doc observed, "Making house calls really was vital in the early '50s. For example, there was a truck that would come out of Wild Cat once a week to get store supplies. They charged 10 cents a ride into town and back. There were always 12 to 15 riders. Folks just did not have cars." So Doc, with his faithful Jeep, simply had to go to them.

TRIGGER FINGER

From the very first appearance of Harold Almond, MD on the local access channel, many in the community tuned in to hear his stories. Nobody was ever disappointed. One evening the following story made my day, as the host and as his son.

Doc recalled a young spunky "school ma'am" from Hacker Valley who was short of stature and soft-spoken but knew she must keep control of her class. This was her first teaching assignment. Two previous teachers gave up frustrated by the tough older hillbilly bullies making classroom discipline nearly impossible. Ever so determined, she'd come to class with a loaded revolver which she laid up on her desk. "The boys were quiet," she reported to Doc.

In her later years she retired to Helvetia where Doc made house calls. Usually he could help her, but one day she presented a puzzling symptom. Her trigger finger would spontaneously flex and spasm. She wrote and shot left handed. As she would write her name, Louise, coming to "o" her fingers would turn white and spasm. Quickly this spread to her hand and to her wrist. She could function by writing with her right hand or by typing. Clearly, though, something was wrong with her proprioception. Doc studied his neurology text books and consulted with colleagues at West Virginia University School of Medicine but could never solve the mystery.

Often as Doc drove by her little white frame house at the edge of Helvetia, he would see her working in her garden. When she'd see him coming she would raise her left arm and index finger toward the passing Jeep, pleading for help. He'd shake his head sadly and drive on up the hill.

Eventually she passed away, taking her malady to her grave. Years later Doc came across an article in his Northwestern University Alumni Journal addressing this diagnosis and treatment effectively. The simple treatment would be splinting. Just as primary grade school children use a pencil expander to improve grasp, so patients suffering from this spasmodic disorder benefit from using a pencil expander as a splint.

When making house calls back on Turkey Bone Mountain where his school ma'am patient was buried, he'd drive past the graveyard in his Jeep. Doc would roll down his window, raise his trigger finger, wave it, and shout, "I know how to treat you now!"

STRAWBERRIES

BRAGGING RIGHTS

"You know," Constance Baston protested.

"No, I don't know," Dr. Harold Almond pleaded.

"Yes, you know," she retorted.

"Ahh, I know!" Doc figured out.

The year was 1988 and for the first time in the history of the Sweetest Strawberry Contest, an Upshur County strawberry grower had won with her entry of Sure Crop.

Doc followed up with a house call to her farm a week after the annual Strawberry Festival. He expected her to be pleased with the $25.00 prize money and her name in the local paper as the supplier of the sweetest berries. In fact she had even defeated the Early Glow variety which is the perennial winner.

The twelve twelve-year old children, six boys and six girls, each with their 12,000 taste buds, did a great job tasting the multiple varieties. The Strawberry Queen and King were on hand as well as various dignitaries so they would know which berry was the sweetest.

But in fact during his visit Doc found Farmer Baston feeling glum. Immediately he realized what to do to cheer her up. The United Methodist preachers were meeting in Conference at West Virginia Wesleyan College, so on the way back to town he stopped over at registration. There a calligrapher was busy making fancy name tags. He requested a scroll inscribed as follows:

LET ALL KNOW THAT
CONSTANCE BASTON
HAS ALL
BRAGGING RIGHTS
AS THE FARMER
GROWING
THE SWEETEST STRAWBERRY
SURE CROP VARIETY
IN WEST VIRGINIA

Framed and proudly displayed in the Baston kitchen hangs this proclamation of bragging rights.

GOOD SOIL

No doubt about it, Doc admired farmers. Whenever he'd make a house call he'd finish up the visit with a request to see the garden. First fruits often served as payment for the doctor bill. He loved strawberries most but also enjoyed blueberries, red raspberries, blackberries and thornless blackberries. On one of his 52 appearances on the TLC TV program he spoke of the benefits of farming.

Lois, his wife of more than 50 years, often rode shotgun on those house calls. They also enjoyed giving talks to church groups combining farming tips and Biblical wisdom. Often the 15th chapter of John, with Jesus describing himself as the true vine, would launch the presentation as Lois led off with scripture.

Doc's cue would be "the true vine." The strawberry plant, he expounded, produces 20 to 22 runners or true vines. Each can be cultivated into a new plant which will then bear two quarts of strawberries. Doc said whenever that happens "then joy is complete."

West Virginia's good soil produced many fruit- bearing varieties of strawberries. Doc and Lois grew them all at their hilltop home. He loved and appreciated all the differences among the varieties:

1—Premier usually remains a standard favorite.
2—Robinson usually is the biggest but is often hollow.
3—Catskill is soft.
4—Dixi is hard.
5—Vermillion is very red and has a wonderful aroma.
6—Cue ball is white.

7—Stoplight is black and ripens quickly over a few days.

8—Sunrise is orange.

9—Early Glow is sweet and ripens over 18 to 19 days.

10—Sparkle grows best in New Jersey where Doc grew up.

11—Fukuda grows best in Japan where he served in the Army – Air Force in the occupation after World War II.

Doc knew his craft. He insisted that on those house calls he could learn much more about a patient than he could ever learn in the office. One thing he realized from his calls was that health and farming went together. People are like fruit: Some folks grow poorly on the wayside, being trodden down; some folks grow between a rock and a hard place, being withered; some folks grow among the thorns and difficulties of life, being choked; and some folks grow in good soil, being fruitful a hundredfold.

INTERESTING ENOUGH

"Doubtless God could have made a sweeter berry; doubtless He never did!" Doc was fond of extolling the strawberry.

"Interesting enough," continued Dr. Harold Almond, teaching in his grand rounds fashion, "when children are twelve years old they have 12,000 taste buds. This is the maximum number a human being will have. So I began a grand experiment back when Maria, our first grand-daughter, was born. She became my sweet strawberry grower. She and I would plant multiple varieties so we could discover which variety in our soil produced the absolutely sweetest berry. Now every year twelve children, twelve years old, serve as the judges in 'The Sweetest Strawberry Contest.' They love it, and they do a great job. Fourteen years straight they picked Early Glow. Of the 1200 varieties, Early Glow is the sweetest except the occasional year when Late Glow is sweeter.

"Interesting enough," Doc enthused, "Dr. Judson, my West Virginia Wesleyan College biology professor, started the Strawberry Festival as a Great Depression self-help program in 1936. He was basically a farmer. He knew our soil grew a superior tasting strawberry. Tuck Farnsworth down at People's Grocery bought 5,000 gallons of strawberries a day and shipped them to an ice cream plant at Uniontown, Pennsylvania. The going price at that time was 65 cents a gallon.

"Interesting enough, Sweetheart is a favorite variety and 'Let Me Call You Sweetheart, I'm in Love With You' is our Strawberry Theme Song."

Yes, if you wanted to know all the interesting facts

about the strawberry and the Strawberry Festival, all you had to do was talk to Doc.

JAGGED EDGE

"Tim, zoom in on this strawberry leaf if you can," Dr. Harold Almond requested of the TV cameraman. "See the jagged edge." Doc loved show and tell; television proved an ideal medium for him. After he retired, when he could no longer bring demonstrations to the nursing station at St. Joseph's Hospital, he welcomed the opportunity the local community access TV channel afforded him. Week after week he'd call up and say he had a good topic for Tender, Loving Care.

What Doc wanted the audience to see was the drop of water that formed on every third jag of the strawberry leaf. "When you see those drops of water, you know the plant is well-hydrated," he explained, clearly excited by this law of nature."The strawberry is 92% water—a higher percentage than even the watermelon.

"Pickens, at the headwaters of the Buckhannon River, is the snow capital of West Virginia, and we have plenty of water here in Buckhannon. When we had our own jagged edge caused by the Great Depression, we had a cash crop in the strawberry. In 1936, the year of the first Strawberry Festival, we had 200 acres of strawberries producing 5,000 gallons of berries a day.

"Night hail is the enemy," Doc continued. "That form of water rather than furthering the strawberry crop can destroy it.

"Frost is worse in the valley, so most strawberry fields are on hilltops and along ridges so as to avoid freezing fog. Now, of course, we can use an all-night water spray on the patch to keep the berries from freezing. So another form of water helps.

"Sweat equity is the final form of water that makes the strawberry grow. We are down from 200 acres planted in the county to probably less than 6 acres." The good doctor shook his head in dismay as the lights faded.

Yes, Doc did know his strawberries.

MORE OR LESS

Always humble, Doc described his role as "more or less, probably less, historian for the Strawberry Festival." He had many footnotes to the official history. There was the 1949 Queen who, ironically enough, was allergic to strawberries. How about the 1969 King who was AWOL in Europe during the Festival? Fate smiles with the runner-up Queen who represented the West Virginia Strawberry Festival in Colorado Springs for the national contest, becoming the Strawberry Queen of Queens in 1957.

"More or less" applies to the beginning of the West Virginia Strawberry Festival as a substitute program for the Buckhannon Lion's Club when the scheduled speaker did not show up. Dr. Judson, Chairperson of Biology at West Virginia Wesleyan College, gained the ears of Kyle Reger, Russell Westfall, Glenn Ford, Tuck Farnsworth, and others. The Festival was born three weeks later in 1936 as a way for "a woman, children, and a hoe" to earn money in the Great Depression from their hill-top garden plots. The May frost would stay in the valley and the soil produced a superior tasting berry.

Doc certainly knew a thing or two about strawberries. He recalled his grandparents' farm in rural New Jersey where he hoed his share of Premier Variety Strawberries. All the strawberries had a common mother and father. In 1906 in southern Vermont the Premier was born. Convent Sisters asked a young man named Howard to go row by row and select the healthiest plant, the sweetest berry and the most abundant crop. Howard 17, also known as Premier, was born. "By chance or by God!" Doc proclaimed as he so often did. The variety proved such a hit it even made the McGuffy Reader.

"By chance or by God," declared Doc again. That's how the variety of strawberry that yields 20% of the United States' crop started. In Virginia farmers were pruning their runners and rejecting the weakest plants. Casually, the unwanted plants were cast aside. Some landed along the coastal waters in the marsh land. The next spring they came to life. For some reason these plants were particularly vigorous. Soon these plants spread down to North Carolina, South Carolina, Georgia, and into Florida. In Plant City, Florida they found a home. Now the "Florida 90" variety produces 20% of all strawberries raised in the USA.

"Strawberry blossoms graced the armor of kings in Europe through the Middle Ages." Actually the berry came about as an international genetic marriage beginning with a plant with a beautiful blossom from Virginia making its way to gardens in England before being transported to Holland. Finally the strawberry plant arrived at King Louis XIV's garden at Versailles, France. At the same time a Frenchman sailed with his ship to study Spanish naval installations in Chile. He fell in love with a particularly beautiful strawberry blossom, so he brought the plant home to France where it also ended up in Louis XIV's garden.

Doc noted with glee that tender loving care resulted in the mating of the two plants and "voila!" the modern, large, juicy strawberry was born.

SALIVARY JUICES

Dr. Harold Almond returned to Buckhannon, West Virginia after military duty which included six months in occupied Japan following World War II. He rejected opportunities to travel later on in his life, from then on stating simply, "I've seen the world."

Whatever else may have happened overseas, he did return with some great stories. One evening on the Tender Loving Care TV program he recalled his encounter with the predominant Japanese strawberry, the Fukuda.

The Fukuda, to hear Doc tell it, is a monster-sized berry. "Just to look at one made my salivary juices just shoot out. But I was afraid to eat one with all those germs." After all, the soil with the human sewage added as fertilizer loved germs.

As a captain and a physician he had the responsibility to inspect the Mess Hall. One of his duties was to taste the food for quality and consistency. Whenever a "Fukuda fit" (akin to a "Big Mac Attack" for Doc) would come, Doc would head for an inspection of the kitchen where he knew there would be boxes of American strawberries. "I taste-tested them and, according to protocol, filed my report with the colonel."

When clearing base to go home he met with the colonel who recognized him and commented that he'd filed a lot of reports about the strawberries. "Yes," Doc explained, "they were ALL good. They saved my life!"

STRAWBERRY MIRACLE

Dr. Harold Almond hurt along with children who were rejected. His empathy for the least, the last, and the lost made him a beloved physician. One evening on the Tender Loving Care TV program he shared a story he told to comfort children whose parents died or were separated by divorce:

Once upon a time there was this beautiful five-petal blossom strawberry plant that was separated from his mother and father in Virginia, North America. He sailed across the rough waves of the Atlantic Ocean. Eventually he was planted in the vast garden of a foreign king, Louis XIV of France. The little strawberry flower did not even speak French. He was so lonely. He cried tears that fell from his jagged leaves. God heard his moans and groans. He used all His love and wisdom to help the little strawberry.

God sent a man who loved strawberries back across the ocean but this time to Chile in South America. There the farmer found a wild and wonderful strawberry flower. He carefully watered it and cared for it on the long journey home to France.

Lo and behold, he planted this new strawberry flower right next to the lonely one from America, and they fell in love. Now a new family of strawberries grew. This time they not only had beautiful blossoms but also delicious berries which would continue for generations to come. They lived happily ever after.

THE HORSE KNOWS THE WAY

A nine-year-old boy helping out his farming grandmother can learn lessons that last a lifetime. Certainly that is what happened with Dr. Harold Almond and his love of the strawberry. One summer in his youth he picked 500 quarts of Premier strawberries and helped deliver them to market by horse and buggy. The family traveled all night, catching some sleep as they traveled. The horse trotted along on his own until he came to a fork in the road, then he'd stop and wake everyone up with a neigh. "Red's" uncle directed the horse to turn left or right. The horse would then continue his journey again, waking everyone up at the next intersection to receive new directions left or right. In the morning the market was reached and all the berries were sold for quite a profit.

When "Red" arrived in Buckhannon in 1939 and the Strawberry Festival was in its third year, he continued his love affair with the strawberry. He was particularly proud of the Sweetest Strawberry Contest and the competition for the best chocolate-covered strawberries, both of which he developed and directed.

When asked what was needed now to make the Strawberry Festival even better he reached back to his youth for the two-part answer:
1—More farmers raising strawberries
2—More education of farmers at Festival time on new growing techniques and new varieties of strawberries.

THE STRAWBERRY EXPERIMENTER

"What's new up at West Virginia University with strawberries?" Doc asked of the agricultural specialist conducting a workshop for small strawberry growers in Upshur County.

"Sengana, Sengana and Stoplight. These are the very latest varieties but no one at W.V.U. has any hands-on experience with these strawberries yet," the professor explained.

With a twinkle in his eye, Doc asked, "Do you want to taste these new varieties today?"

"Yes, but that's impossible."

"Not at all. Harley Tenney has them ripe and ready in his patch near Mt. Washington," Doc beamed. A short Jeep ride later the Professor and Doc were in strawberry heaven.

From that day on, university professors always stopped up to see what was new in Harley Tenney's strawberry patch every time they came to town. Harley grew ten different varieties in his 1500-plant patch. He knew that for the first grower of 25 or more plants with new variety and ripe strawberries, there is a $25.00 prize during the Strawberry Festival. He figured he'd raise the varieties nobody else knew anything about and walk away with the prize money every year.

His wife, who worked in the newborn nursery at St. Joseph's Hospital, helped him out for the grueling two weeks of harvest. She confessed that her back grew so tired she was glad to get back from her vacation to work.

But sure enough, her husband would walk away with that coveted prize.

WEED EATING DUCKS

Strawberry King Maurice Brady of Abbott, West Virginia, kept ducks in his strawberry patch as they were excellent weed eaters. Of course, they had to be out when the berries ripened. Fattened by plenty of eating, they would make good victuals. Unfortunately, "Raynard, the Red Fox" came over the fence and ate the ducks.

Other more practical ways to keep down weeds includes raising soy beans and corn in the patch for two years before planting berries. The corn would be harvested but the soy beans would be plowed under to enrich the soil. The next year, a thin plastic sheeting would be placed over the ground. Methyl bromide gas would then be injected into the soil twelve inches apart and twelve inches deep. The soil would remain sterile and weed-free for several years following.

And of course there is always the old-fashioned way to rid your garden of weeds: get out in the hot sun and start pulling!

LET ME CALL YOU SWEETHEART
BY
LINDA BOOTH CORONET

Doc had a great sense of community pride when he spoke of Buckhannon's annual Strawberry Festival. Following is the theme song for the popular festival:

Well God created berries to grow upon the vine,
Sweet strawberries that taste divine.
One is called the Sweetheart, a favorite of mine,
Princess of the berries, the farmers' valentine.

I love your little runners and your little baby feet,
Your little yellow freckles, your blossoms sweet
Your little red pajamas and your little cap of green
Oh, you're my little Sweetheart, the fairest I have seen.

I love to gather Sweethearts before the morning heat,
And take them to the table and settle down to eat.
They go with cream and sugar, they go with cream of wheat.
They go with Grandma's shortcake, a very noble treat.

When the time is ready following the snow
You can plant some Sweethearts and help them grow.
Nurse them like a nanny and sing a little rhyme.
The nursery will soon be crowded at berry
picking time.

Let me call you Sweetheart, I'm in love with you,
Sweet and red as rubies, fresh as dew.
You are the finest berry the farmer ever grew.
Let me call you Sweetheart, I'm in love with you.

STRAWBERRY BENEDICTION

Let the color of these strawberries remind us of the beauty of creation.

Let the taste of these strawberries remind us of the sweetness of a fruitful life.

Let the size of these strawberries remind us of the time and effort given by the growers.

Let these strawberries remind us of lives that are enriched as we share with each other.

Bless these strawberries as symbols of lives that are pure and sweet.

Printed with permission of Reverend Steve Engel and the Strawberry Association
1987 Strawberry Festival

ST. JOSEPH'S HOSPITAL   BUCKHANNON, W. VA.

OB-H873

ST. JOSEPH'S HOSPITAL

A GLIMPSE OF HEAVEN

Dr. Harold Almond had really enjoyed practicing medicine in the old Barlow Mansion where he started the first emergency room. Space being at a premium, the Sisters who ran the hospital did not want to give up a room. They set a high bar for the young energetic redhead—the ER must produce at least $6.00 per day.

In 1964 St. Joseph's Hospital moved into their new building. Now the hospital had too much space. Frankly, patients were staying away. Doc puzzled over this and thought of a biblical parallel. Previously there had been such a press of folks, just like the healing of the paralytic when everyone was so desperate to be close to the Great Physician that four friends let their paralyzed buddy down through the roof. When Jesus saw their faith, he said to the paralytic, "Your sins are forgiven. Arise, and take up your bed and walk." Now, however, with plenty of room and doctors available, patients were nowhere to be found.

Doc cogitated for a while before reasoning that the doctors and staff of St. Joseph's needed to have a health fair, giving away their services for preventive health screens. Strengthening faith and trust would be vital for the success of the new hospital.

What a grand day the health fair turned out to be. Everyone in town was involved, with volunteers ranging from the nursing students at West Virginia Wesleyan College to various church and civic groups. The Roman Catholic Bishop visited from Wheeling to bless the new building, declaring, "Healing is a glimpse of Heaven."

MAKING OF A PHYSICIAN

Greenbrier remembers:

Rarely does a lad have such great mentors. Boy, was I on top of the world. Dad was letting me go into surgery with him. He said since I was twelve I was old enough. The night before the big day I could hardly sleep; I was so excited.

We drove together in the old green Jeep up the narrow hospital hill road, making the sharp turn to the back of the Barlow Mansion/St. Joseph's Hospital. Inside the smells were strong, permeating my nostrils with the scents of rubbing alcohol and soap. Upon entering the old-fashioned elevator with gate doors, I felt a thrill of joy as we clanged up the two floors ever so slowly.

In the small hospital room with its sloping white walls, I spotted the baby in her mother's arms. Dad and I inspected the harelip and he talked to the parents about the operation. The baby appeared so tiny, and I was amazed that Dr. Basil Page could operate on such a small lip.

Soon we were scrubbing in and gowning up. Dr. Jake Huffman entered the operating suite to set up the anesthesia. He chatted amicably of his and Kathleen's recent trip to faraway Tahiti. Mrs. Smith, the scrub nurse, helped me tie my gown. I felt awkward but important at the same time.

Now Dr. Basil Page arrived. He asked about my mother and my sisters. Then he began an anatomy lesson of the lip. I understood he'd make a flap and sew it over the middle of the philtrum. Dr. Huffman sang a verse or two of "I've Been Working on the Railroad" as he made the final preparations with gauze and an opened ether bottle.

Now we were underway. The mask seemed so confining over my own nose and mouth. The baby cooed and then slept. Dr. Page cut a bit and Dad sponged the blood away. Suddenly the ether smelled so strong. I began to sweat profusely. Then I slumped to the floor.

Alas, I had fainted.

Afterward, Dr. Page, Dr. Huffman, and Dad all declared that they had fainted or nearly fainted when they had first been exposed to blood. "Remember empathy—feeling your patient's suffering—is the first lesson of learning medicine," Dad said. "And you certainly did that!" he laughed.

TARGET PRACTICE

"Dad, St. Joseph's ER is on the line," I called into the bedroom where he was having a bit of shuteye after being up all night with a delivery.

Dad took the phone and frowned as he listened to Sister Agistine.

"Yes, a shooting. I'll be right up," Dad responded.

"Honey, we'll eat Thanksgiving Dinner together when you get home," Mom offered, always a gracious and patient doctor's wife.

"Greenbrier, come with me. These kids are your age," Dad requested.

As we entered the side door of the old Barlow Mansion/ St. Joseph's Hospital, even I at only 5 feet had to duck to avoid bumping my head on the low-hanging water pipes. The place was not only quiet but solemn; it felt eerie. We entered a small room that served as the ER. Sister stood by in the corner wrapping her arms around a sobbing woman. Down the hall toward the main entrance I could see a man with his head bowed low, shoulders slumped, and a boy about ten years old squatted on the floor by him.

Dad stepped to the examination table in the middle of the room. He turned back the sheet to reveal a small boy with an ashen face. I peered closer as Dad examined his chest where a bullet had apparently entered his chest on the left and then out on the right. There was no life in him.

Dad shook his head. He approached Sister and the woman. Grasping the woman with both hands he said softly, "I'm so sorry."

Slowly I followed Dad down the hall where he asked the man what had happened. "The boys were target practicing. Johnny stepped right out in front of Billy."

Dad turned to the boy and quietly said, "I lost my brother when I was about your age. It hurts so much."

We stepped into the little office with the switchboard. I heard him tell the sheriff it was an accident. Then he helped me with my coat, rubbing my hair with his warm hands. "Button up, it's getting cold out there."

THE LITTLE ONES

"The happiest part of medicine is delivering babies," Dr. Harold Almond declared. He remained modest of his own accomplishments. But he acknowledged that three physicians are pictured on the delivery room wall at St. Joseph's Hospital in Buckhannon: Jake Huffman, MD; Bob Chamberlain, MD; and Harold Almond, MD.

Together they delivered 12,000 babies.

"But the greatest among us was Sister Heriberta." Doc's eyes sparkled as he recalled her feats of tender loving care. "She was the best of the best." For 20 years Doc had chaired the Morbidity and Mortality Committee for the hospital. He quickly realized that the newborn nursery under Sister's care saved the lives of more premature babies than any other hospital in West Virginia.

"She was a little lady with a big heart," Doc noted. Whatever success she had she gave God the glory. "Healing is His work!" Sister often proclaimed.

Doc remembered with much respect the time he delivered the eleventh child of a poor family from Czar. The "preemie" weighed only one pound, twelve ounces. (A term baby at average birth weight is seven pounds, one ounce for a girl and seven pounds, two ounces for a boy.) Sister prayed and tenderly cared for the baby who soon grew strong. Then, as if to challenge God himself, in eleven months the mother returned delivering her twelfth child, also a "preemie," and also weighing one pound, twelve ounces. Sister prayed all the more and tenderly nursed this baby to health as well.

Sister Heriberta's formula consisted of three goals as part of her tender loving care:

1—keep the baby's temperature up
2—keep the baby's stomach full
3—keep the baby clean

The "little ones" slept in foot lockers with an electric light bulb dangling down. When the temperature went down, the bulb went on. Often a feeding tube would be needed as the baby could not swallow. Oxygen came from a tank with a simple funnel to direct the flow toward the baby. The babies always were very clean—and very well-loved.

WEBSTER COUNTY'S FORESTS PRODUCED THE LARGEST HARDWOOD TREE EXHIBITED AT THE CHICAGO WORLD'S FAIR IN 1933

WEST VIRGINIA'S VERTICAL RANGE IS 4,600 FEET—ONE OF THE WIDEST VARIATIONS OF ANY STATE IN THE UNION.....THE HIGHEST POINT IS SPRUCE KNOB, PENDLETON COUNTY, 4,680 FEET ABOVE SEA LEVEL—THE LOWEST THE BED OF THE POTOMAC RIVER AT HARPERS FERRY, ONLY 260 FEET ABOVE THE SEA

LUMBERMEN SAY THE LARGEST TREE EVER GROWN IN WEST VIRGINIA WAS A POPLAR, CUT SEVERAL YEARS AGO ON OLD LICK RUN, NEAR HOLLY, WEBSTER COUNTY....THE TREE WAS CUT BY THE PARDEE-CURTAIN LUMBER COMPANY AND MEASURED 33 FEET IN CIRCUMFERENCE

7

Lowell Talbott

APPALACHIAN TRAIL

APPALACHIAN TRAIL

Remote for detachment
Narrow for chosen company
Winding for leisure
Lonely for contemplation
It beckons not merely north and south
But upward for the body, mind, and soul of
man.

>Myron Avery
>Appalachian Trail
>president, 1931 - 1952

Dr. Harold Almond often spoke of lessons learned as a young man blazing the Appalachian Trail. First, he learned the value of volunteer endeavor since the AT, as the Appalachian Trail is known, represents the greatest volunteer effort in the world.

He experienced the call of the wild having hiked and camped from Harper's Ferry, West Virginia to Mount Katahdin, Maine on two different occasions.

Doc developed a love of storytelling around the Adirondack Shelter campfire at the end of a long hike. As a tour guide and cook he took many three-month tours, being responsible for sixteen to eighteen novices.

Above the tree line while hiking Mt. Washington, Doc learned the value of communication. The AT is marked for hikers with red paint on rock painted over with a two by six inch mark of white paint. Doc recalled snow in August on Mt. Washington and Thunderstorm Junction. Piles of rock are everywhere but one with a pole in the middle marks the AT. Without a careful blaze, a person's life is in danger.

Getting out of a tight place was a lesson learned at Moose Notch, where a hiker must take off his backpack and crawl over, under, and through massive rocks.

All in all, Doc's Appalachian Trail experiences prepared him well for life as a country doctor.

NUDIST COLONY

Hiking the Appalachian Trail north of the Delaware Water Gap and heading toward Bear Mountain Bridge across the Hudson River, "Red" had a most revealing encounter. Twice a year he and other boy scouts painted the two by six inch white AT symbol at every turn keeping the trail well-marked in New Jersey. Also, routine maintenance meant cutting under-brush back from the trail.

Coming over a rise on the trail the scouts' eyes nearly popped out. A nudist colony was under construction, and appropriately enough the folks had only their birthday suits on. "Red" approached the colony and with wisdom beyond his years told them they were building in the wrong place. He predicted they would be gone in a year. Taking his advice the wrong way, the colonist told "Red" they had a right to be there and they had no intention of leaving, AT or no AT.

Just as Doc had predicted, the next time the scouts repainted the trail, the nudist colony was no more. What "Red" had really been telling them was that the site they had chosen was beside a swamp. When the mosquitoes all came out to eat, the nudists would be history.

OUTSMARTING PORCUPINES AND OTHER VARMINTS

Dad loved to reminisce. One evening on the TLC TV program he recalled his days working as a fire lookout:

Living in a fire tower on Glastenbury Mountain along the Long Trail in Vermont taught me to be smarter than Mother Nature. Bears never bothered me. Moose piqued my curiosity. The worst varmints, hands down, were the porcupines. At the Long Trail Lodge ninety miles north of the Massachusetts border, the porcupines came right inside the restaurant. The automobile-driving tourists were softies, playing right into those porcupines' schemes. The people missed a meal or two after being outsmarted into handing their food over, willingly or not, to the darned porcupines. The search for food is simply the survival of the fittest, the porcupines coming out on top in this particular battle.

Cutting ferns around the fire tower and along the trail I came upon a free meal. There were wild duck eggs all around Half-Mile Lake. Boy did my salivary juices flow. But when I cracked one, the egg was rotten. Then another, rotten too. And again, rotten. Those wild ducks just lay eggs and forgot them. I returned to the fire tower frustrated.

Rain fell all night. It matched my mood; I was sad. Then about two in the morning I awoke. Eureka! The next day I went back to the lake and drew a circle in the sand. Then I took all the eggs out of the circle. Later I returned to see five fresh eggs laid within the circle. Victory! The eggs tasted strong but were great with bacon. Survival of the fittest, right?

SCOUTING PREPARES FOR LIFE

Hiking and camping thrilled little twelve-year-old "Red" from the day he joined Boy Scouts in 1927. He loved the telling of stories around the campfire, too. One evening after hiking the Long Trail in Vermont the stories turned scary about bears and snakes.

Finally turning in, "Red" felt a long snake in his sleeping bag with him. While he was frightened, he knew from what his Scout Master taught that there were no poisonous snakes above the Massachusetts/Vermont border. He figured the cold blooded friend just wanted warmed up. Nevertheless he did escort him out of his sleeping bag.

"Red" applied and was in the running to accompany Admiral Byrd on his historic exploration of the South Pole. The Admiral invited Boy Scouts to apply, as he trusted a Scout would be a good addition to his expedition. Paul Sykes, an Eagle Scout, won the honor. He brought back three pairs of penguins which for years were the chief attraction at the Washington D.C. Zoo. For only $5.00, a person could ride a train from New York City to Washington D.C. and back to see the penguins. Sykes did mapping for the Admiral and figured out the formula for what is now called "chill factor." He correctly concluded that air temperature, measured in Fahrenheit, combined with wind speed, measured in miles per hour, would accurately measure how dangerous is the loss of body heat. Antarctica had windy, snowy days that were bitterly cold. Though "Red" wanted to go, Paul was a good choice.

A big chill for "Red," now Doc, came one night on a house call trip to Silica. This was the only time Doc turned back unable to reach his patient. He left about 10:00 pm with his friend and neighbor, Raymond Lockwood. The wind was blustery and the blowing snow blinding. The little green Jeep ran right into a tree that had fallen across the road near Mt. Etna. After cutting the tree up, the duo drove on toward Helvetia. There the industrious Swiss-Germans had already plowed their own roads. But after climbing the mountain out of the deep, upper Buckhannon River valley, the snow was so deep the Jeep would not even drive forward downhill. Backing down to Stine's store, Doc gassed up, drank coffee, and slept. In the morning breakfast was cheerfully served to the stranded duo. By 4:00 pm the snow was still falling.

"I never thought I'd get out in such a wild wonderful primitive place like West Virginia when I first joined Scouts, but I loved it!"

TENSION LINE

One night on the Tender Loving Care TV program, the following conversation occurred between Doc and his son Greenbrier:

Greenbrier: A physician helps his patient through the dark night of illness. How do you speak peace and quiet the deepest fears?

Harold: I remind patients of what they know to be true. In these West Virginia Hills we have a solid foundation.

Greenbrier: Let's do an exercise, Dad. I'll give a verse of the 121st Psalm which speaks to our help coming from the hills. You respond with a word of comfort as you do so well. "I will lift up my eyes unto the hills, from whence cometh my help."

Harold: My hills are my Appalachian Trail experiences that sustain body, mind and soul. I remember looking through the "retrospect-scope."

Greenbrier: "My help cometh from the Lord, which made heaven and earth."

Harold: God created the West Virginia Hills. He created us. The whole world is in his hands.

Greenbrier: "He will not suffer thy foot to be moved: he that keepeth thee will not slumber. Behold, he that keepeth Israel shall neither slumber nor sleep."

Harold: Even when hiking up a muddy foot trail along a mountain creek to see a patient in his home carrying a doctor bag, I feel sure footed. Usually I whistle. I made many house calls at night because that is when my patient needed me most.

Greenbrier: "The Lord is thy keeper: the Lord is thy shade upon thy right hand. The sun shall not smite thee by day, nor the moon by night."

Harold: I remind my patient of the comfort from the hills that God created. I remind myself of my days hiking the Appalachian Trail. Those granite mountains in Vermont, New Hampshire, and Maine suffered through the Ice Age and are still there. While the wind may blow on so hard that trees grow out longitudinally instead of upward, they still grow. I've seen Spruce Trees with six foot long limbs running along the ground.

Greenbrier: "The Lord shall preserve thee from all evil: he shall preserve thy soul. The Lord shall preserve thy going out and thy coming in from this time forth, and even for evermore."

Harold: The Lord preserves beauty and vitality in the harshest conditions. The three prettiest flowers God has ever created grow on the tension line. That is a demarcation in the highest, most rugged granite peaks. On one side is beautiful life hanging on bravely and on the other side is bare granite, barren of all life. Those little flowers are wonderful. The Artic Azalea is red. The Lap Land Roseberry is royal purple. The Diaspea is white. As the Mountaineer says "upon my word" I've walked miles along the tension line and those little red, purple and white flowers grow and grow and grow. We certainly can look unto the hills for help!

FOND OF FISHING AND HUNTING- IS A MEMBER OF NATIONAL ASSOCIATION OF SHERIFFS - ODD FELLOWS - K OF P - CHAMBER OF COMMERCE AND LION'S CLUB. ALSO ACTIVE MEMBER METHODIST CHURCH.

WAS BORN IN UPSHUR COUNTY IN 1883. GREW UP ON FATHER'S FARM- ATTENDED FREE SCHOOL., COMPLETING EDUCA -- TION AT WEST VIRGINIA WESLEYAN COLLEGE, BUCKHANNON. TAUGHT SCHOOL SIX YEARS.

IS NOW SUCCESSFULLY SERVING SECOND TERM AS SHERIFF OF UPSHUR COUNTY. HE IS MARRIED AND THE FATHER OF FOUR CHILDREN - THREE BOYS AND ONE GIRL. ~ ~ ~

WAS IN LUMBER BUSINESS IN FAYETTE CO. 9 YEARS- IN LITTLE WASHINGTON, OHIO 1 YEAR- THEN IN UPSHUR CO. UNTIL ELECT- ED SHERIFF IN 1924. ~ ~

from photo ~Morgan Bailey~

Pictorial Biographies—No. 6

WEST VIRGINIA WESLEYAN COLLEGE

A MOST REWARDING LIFE

Dr. Harold Almond grieved for town and gown upon the death of Professor Bill Hallam at age 92. He used the Tender Loving Care TV program to recall the good professor's summation of a full life: "My life here has been most rewarding. I've loved it."

And he was loved in return.

Doc recalled that Professor Hallam was the first secretary of Buckhannon's Strawberry Festival. He built the first analog computer in West Virginia and also built a glider that flew over West Virginia Wesleyan College. For forty-five years he taught practically every physics and math course at the college. During many of the early Depression years he was the only math professor. His ham radio handle, W8LD, was known in all 50 states and in 50 countries. As timer for all Wesleyan basketball and football games, Professor Hallam never missed cheering on the teams. In later years he represented the college faculty as a "graybeard," and an honorary doctorate granted by Wesleyan sweetened his senior years.

WBUC radio's chief engineer, Phil Phillips, fondly recalled on the TLC TV program that evening how "Prof" knew Morse Code better than anyone. He could receive or send 45 letters a minute while carrying on a general conversation.

For Doc's sake Greenbrier recalled Professor Hallam telling about the early days when Dr. Almond, a.k.a. "Red," had returned to Buckhannon to practice medicine. The Hallam's had called for him to make a house call. Doc arrived promptly. He said "yes, sir" and "yes, ma'am." They noted he was the most polite doctor they had ever met.

Dr. Harold Almond finished the moving eulogy with the recollection that during World War II, Professor Hallam had traveled to Wright-Patterson Air Force Base to suggest West Virginia Wesleyan College as a perfect training site. The military came and liked what they saw. Agnes Howard Hall became a military dorm along with two additional gray buildings built on campus. For years after the war, the student center of Wesleyan, a.k.a. The SCOW, was located in one of those buildings. The other functioned as a classroom and college kindergarten.

Indeed, Professor Bill Hallam lived a most rewarding life.

ACROSS THE TABLE DIAGNOSIS

Harold and Lois Almond met and fell in love at West Virginia Wesleyan College. Anticipating their 50th wedding anniversary with a chance to establish a living memorial, the Harold and Lois Flanagan Almond Scholarship at W.V.W.C. became a reality. In fact Wesleyan honored both Harold and Lois with the Alumni Award. College Homecoming each fall remained a highlight of their year.

One year Doc discovered one of his F.B.I. Top 10 diseases right before his eyes. A wife of an alum had a persistent drooping eyelid which caught Doc's attention. Then as she began to eat he noticed she chewed her food less and less, even spitting out some of it. Finally, ever so casually he asked, "How long have you had Myasthenia Gravis?"

Amazed, she described the course of her illness, concluding that it took extended visits to four neurologists to make the diagnosis that a country doctor made across a dinner table.

GOOD CHEMISTRY

Rarely do a professor and student bond so well as Nicholas Hyma and Harold Almond did. Harold remembered with glee in his eye and broad smile on his face that Nicholas Hyma had invited him to come back to Wesleyan and teach physical chemistry. The prospect of being close to his mentor meant everything to the young physician looking at all options including practicing as a company doctor at Cass, West Virginia or possibly staying in the military twelve more years adding to the eight garnered with World War II.

Bonding came early. Harold had been an excellent student of chemistry at Wesleyan. Later when Harold was in trouble at Northwestern University School of Medicine in his freshman year with his bold correction of the head of the internal medicine department, he wired back to Nicholas Hyma for support. Dr. Hyma had taught his young charge well. Boyle's Law *did* apply to Triple Sulfa IV Antibiotic pharmacotherapy even though the medical school professor did not believe it. "Stick to your guns," Dr. Hyma wired back. Harold did. All was well. He earned his first "A" in medical school and many lives were saved, beginning with patients in the 7,200 bed Cook County Charity Hospital.

After Doc returned to West Virginia, Nicholas Hyma enjoyed making house calls with his former student. Fondly reflecting, Harold recalled one all-night adventure (one of many) that began with a house call thirty miles to Newlon, then on a few country miles to Selbyville, followed by a seven-mile midnight run and stop to Helvetia, continuing on seven more miles in the wee hours to Hemlock and ending up at Ten Mile just as dawn broke. Both men had full loads of work waiting as they returned to town tired but satisfied. Bond they did.

When the polio vaccine needed to be given in rural communities, Nicholas Hyma was always available to help. He enjoyed playing doctor.

For the final act of Nicholas Hyma's life, his friend Harold was there too. After suffering an acute anterior wall myocardial infarction and being hospitalized at Elkins, Nicholas was transferred to St. Joseph's Hospital. He appeared to be getting well. In fact he graded papers in his room when Harold stopped by. There was no chest pain. Harold said he had a house call to make at Volga. Both wished they could go together. A quick check on a baby in the nursery and Harold would be off. While he was in the nursery, word came that Nicholas wanted to see him again. When Harold returned, Nicholas Hyma said, "Tell them at the College to carry on!"

"Yes, yes," Harold responded, puzzled by his friend's words.

Hours later returning from his call, Harold learned from the local gas station attendant that Nicholas Hyma had died.

"How did he know he would die and I did not know?" Harold still puzzled years later.

MIDDLE NAME "MUD"—ALMOST

For seven years Doc served his alma mater, West Virginia Wesleyan College, as its college physician. He enjoyed the role, including the opportunity to attend basketball games. One winter evening Wesleyan was in a see-saw game with Fairmont State. Ten minutes remained. Emotions ran high with cheers and boos on every play.

Suddenly Fairmont's star forward slipped and fell hard, dislocating his shoulder. Doc responded by coming to his aid amid cheers. He knew the maneuver of cocking the arm across the chest and pulling hard. The shoulder reduced. Now more cheers but also some groans.

The player sat out a sequence but soon rejoined his team. He shot accurately and the game continued to see-saw. Finally the buzzer sounded with Wesleyan triumphing by one point. As Doc left the arena a fan reminded him that he could have waited ten more minutes to reduce the dislocation. After all, the patient was the opposing team's star player. Doc just shook his head, saying that the longer a physician waits, the harder the reduction becomes. He then realized his name almost became Dr. Harold "Mud" Almond.

UNSOLVED MYSTERY OF THE CHURCH BELL TOWER DEATH

Being a deaf organist as well as a chemistry professor is enough to deal with. But then to know there has been a death in the bell tower of the church is too much. Always with a twinkle in his eye and a ready smile, Nicholas Hyma knew he could deduct the answer through scientific reasoning.

Look at the facts: a brown/green ring around the cornea, an unsteady gait and then a fall, and a penchant for Evangelical grape juice or wine.

Dr. Nicholas Hyma accepted the challenge to solve the mystery with his soft-spoken, modest manner. He consulted his former student, now physician, Dr. Perkins, who had arrived at West Virginia Wesleyan College so poor his one pair of pants was falling apart. Professor tailored his own pants down to size and presented them to Perkins, a friend for life.

The physician informed the professor that the unsteady gait can signify malnourishment as in poverty or in alcoholics who drink rather than eat.

Dr. Hyma then met with his good friend, attorney Myron Hymes, whose daughter's name graced the label of Hyma's world famous "Carol Ann Hand Lotion." The attorney informed the professor that Upshur was a dry county but moonshine still abounded. Poisoning with heavy metals was probable.

Finally, he turned to young "Red" Almond, the new young doctor just back from World War II. Doc loved syndromes and mysteries. The brown/green ring around the cornea must represent copper metabolism problems or poisoning, he informed the professor.

Now Nicholas Hyma's mind went to work. One of the best teachers Wesleyan ever attracted offered up a simple analysis which autopsy confirmed. Amazingly Nicholas Hyma performed the autopsy, too, as he did have one year of medical school as a young man. It was determined that the man died of copper poisoning from copper tubing in his moonshine still from the acidic chemical reaction of grapes and copper. The idea of seeking refuge in the Evangelical United Brethren Church bell tower spoke to his concrete interpretation of scripture: "Wine is a mocker, strong drink is raging: whosoever is deceived thereby is not wise." Professor Hyma's eyes twinkled as he laughed, "The dead man could not be a Wesleyan student for they all took sobriety pledges and are all wise."

WESLEYAN'S SQUIRRELS

"Hi fellers!" John Huber would always greet the male students when he served food in the college cafeteria. On the other hand he knew all the girls by name. John was working his way through West Virginia Wesleyan College. He stayed on the third floor of President McCuskey's home, keeping up the coal-fired furnace in winter.

"Red" and John decided Wesleyan would be better off if there were squirrels around campus. For some reason there were none, even though trees abounded. So they visited the French Creek Game Farm and brought back two squirrels. As they were releasing them among the Wesleyan oaks, one squirrel bit John's thumb. It looked horrible, Doc recalled.

John declared in faith, "And we know that all things work together for good to them that love God, to them who are the called according to his purpose."

Little did he know how mysterious God's ways can be. He went on to Garrett Theological Seminary in Chicago as "Red" went on to Northwestern University Medical School also in Chicago. Both joined the military service, but John had some difficulty getting accepted as a chaplain. He was told that he did not have any real-life work experience. When he offered that he had worked for the railroad briefly as a laborer, the recruitment officer spotted his thumb and commented, "Yes, that is a horrible looking thumb, you must have worked hard. Come on in." After service as a military chaplain, he went on to be the first chaplain at Chicago's O'Hare Airport.

"Red" returned to the squirrels of Wesleyan as a

practicing physician. He fondly called his grandchildren by the pet name "fellers." Little Ginger loved it and would always greet everyone with "Hi fellers!"

THE FAMED KATE'S MOUNTAIN CLOVER IS FOUND NOWHERE BUT ON KATE'S MOUNTAIN, NEAR WHITE SULPHUR SPRINGS

SINCE ABOUT THE YEAR 1760 FRASER'S SEDGE HAS BEEN KNOWN TO BOTANISTS BY ONE SPECIMEN WHICH WAS FOUND BY MATHIAS KIN, ECCENTRIC DUTCH NURSERYMAN .... HIS NOTES DESCRIBED THE LOCATION OF HIS DISCOVERY AS "DAIGER VELLY IN TER VILDERNESS". RECENTLY A WASHINGTON D.C. BOTANIST, THINKING KIN MIGHT HAVE MEANT THE TYGART VALLEY, SEARCHED THERE AND FOUND THE PLANT GROWING

THIS STRANGELY SHAPED SWEET POTATO WAS GROWN BY MRS. STACEY ANN SMITH OF ABBOT, UPSHUR COUNTY

Lowell Talbott

PICKENS,
HELVETIA,
AND
UPSHUR COUNTY

A HAND SHAKE

Pickens is a remarkable place.

Maybe it's the snow. After all, it is the snow capital of West Virginia, with more than 202 inches averaged there each year. On the 4th of July, 1891 the B & O Rails reached Pickens in the snow.

Maybe it's the elevation. While West Virginia is the most elevated state in the east with an average height above sea level of 1,500 feet, Pickens stands at 2,900 feet with Turkey Bone Mountain overshadowing at 3,900 feet.

Maybe it's the religious dedication of the elders. Consider Peter and Ida Swint. One son became a Roman Catholic Bishop and four daughters became nuns. The other brothers and sisters led lives of tenacity and strength.

What better story to describe the character of Pickens than to recall the building of the new brick Catholic church. Bishop Swint and a young priest met with his master carpenter friend, Rudolph Zumbach, going over the details of construction:

Bishop: Rudolph, can you move the stain glass windows from the old church to the new?

Rudolph: Yes.

Bishop: Rudolph, can you move the pews from the old church to the new?

Rudolph: Yes.

Bishop: Rudolph, can you move the altar from the old church to the new?

Rudolph: Yes.

And then, a hand shake.

The young priest was puzzled and uneasy as he and Bishop Swint walked away. "Sir, you did not get a cost estimate for labor or material. You did not sign any contract."

The old bishop smiled. "You do not know the way work is done in Pickens. Not only will the work be done for a cost less than you might estimate, but the work will be superior to what you might expect."

Later at the dedication of the new chapel, the young priest exclaimed to Dr. Harold Almond, "The workmanship is outstanding and done for far less than I would have ever thought possible. The Bishop certainly knows the best way."

I WISH I WOULD HAVE KNOWN MORE

George Rashid, the leper patient of Dr. James Cunningham, presented quite a challenge to the country doctor. As he told Dr. Harold Almond, his personal physician, during a house call made when the senior doctor was 100 years old, "I wish I would have known more." Apparently he did not even know how infectious leprosy might be. "I just did everything I could for my patient."

Doc loved to solve mysteries. During West Virginia University's School of Medicine's orientation day, Dean Robert D'Alessandri asked him to relate three of the stories from his book, *Stories of a West Virginia Doctor*. Doc urged the group of future doctors to "Keep an FBI list of the ten most wanted diseases. Be on the lookout for them. Read about them. Be prepared." Doc then expounded on Dr. Cunningham's experience as a B & O physician at the end of the rail line.

For the three months that George Rashid lived in Pickens, Dr. Cunningham ensured that he had a house, food, and tender loving care. President Teddy Roosevelt sent the Pickens physician a revolver with instructions to protect the leper, as the President did not want any international crisis with the country of Lebanon, the country from which George had emigrated. Dr. Cunningham did just that. He stood his ground and risked his reputation and life for his patient.

During his account of the story on the Tender Loving Care TV program, Dr. Harold Almond stated that years later medical science discovered that care providers of leprosy patients do not get the disease. Furthermore, the scientific breakthrough in treatment came when it was discovered that the organism could be grown on a mouse paw and in a South American anteater's belly. He noted that there is triple therapy for leprosy, yet it remains one of the most common infectious diseases worldwide. He concluded his telling of the personal tale of Dr. Cunningham and his patient with the universal desire of every physician: "I wish I would have known more."

ONE OF THE HAPPIEST PEOPLE I'VE EVER MET

Dr. Harold Almond loved to lift up Dr. James L. Cunningham during his appearances on the Tender Loving Care TV program. One night he revealed why: "He was quite simply one of the happiest people I've ever met!" he exclaimed. "He was the Albert Schweitzer of Pickens."

"One is only happy when one has learned how to serve," Doc paraphrased Dr. Schweitzer. Certainly this was true for Dr. Cunningham, who initially taught school in Hacker Valley before going on to study medicine in Baltimore. Actually he had joined the Navy but returned to his beloved Pickens before planning to head out for high seas adventure and the Spanish-American War. But there was a dreaded measles epidemic in the community prompting Dr. Cunningham to ask the Navy to extend his leave. The rest is history.

"Dr. Cunningham wore out 14 horses making house calls over a 65-year period of service to the mountain community of Pickens and the surrounding farms," Doc spoke with amazement about Dr. Cunningham's feats. "He delivered 3,600 babies in the home and did not lose a single mother."

"One of the high privileges in my own practice was to be Dr. Cunningham's personal physician in his final years. He remained alert up to the age of 102." Doc recalled learning the secret of his practice philosophy during one of his own house calls to the good doctor's residence in Pickens. "Dr. Cunningham quite simply had a patient to take care of and he took care of him!"

When asked to describe his own secret of success Doc just as simply declared, "I always tried to exceed my patient's expectations!" And how did that work out? Any regrets? "Not at all! All I wanted in life was to practice medicine and I got my chance," explained one of the happiest people I've ever met.

PIONEER SPIRIT

One evening I asked my father, "Dad, what are the personality traits that made Dr. Cunningham such a great physician?"

Dr. Harold Almond scratched his head, closed his eyes in reflection, and then characterized Dr. Cunningham with three stories:

Mabel, his daughter, had told Doc of the time Dr. Cunningham returned home on horseback on a cold, icy snowy night way past midnight. He realized that he was frozen to his horse and could not move or get off the steed. He began to shout to awaken his wife and two daughters but to no avail. To get closer he ordered the horse to climb the front steps to the porch. From there the horse pranced loudly and the doctor yelled out into the frozen night until his sleeping family awoke. Mabel recalled that she needed to get an ax and break the layered ice encasing her father before he could dismount and come inside to thaw out.

Continuing to reflect, Dr. Harold Almond remembered making a house call to Pickens when the good doctor was 98 years old. Lo and behold, Dr. Cunningham was up on his shed roof tarring it for water proofing. Genuinely alarmed, Dr. Almond yelled up at the top of his lungs ordering him off. But Dr. Cunningham just cocked his head, cupping his hand over his ear, shaking his head that he did not hear, and continued to tar the roof, not coming down until the task was completed.

Upon my word, Doc exclaimed, at 99 years old Dr. Cunningham hitchhiked from Pickens to Webster Springs and then home again. When asked how he could ever think of doing such a thing, Dr. Cunningham simply replied that it was a lot easier to hitchhike by automobile than to ride by horse and buggy.

SADDLE BAGS

Dr. Harold Almond loved teaching visitors to the Roberts-Cunningham Museum all about the tools of the physician-surgeon who used them for nearly 65 years. He thrilled children with tales of the almost legend-like Dr. Cunningham "wearing out fourteen horses but always having three in the stable ready to go."

In the saddle bags which fastened around the horse's abdomen behind Dr. Cunningham he kept supplies such as his sterile surgical tools. After all, the good doctor might be called upon to amputate the leg of a B & O railway section-hand underwater.

There was the Typhoid Fever epidemic of 1914-1915 when Dr. Cunningham cared for 1,200 people. The secret of the remarkably low 2% mortality was "fluids, fluids, fluids." Those saddle bags contained everything the good doctor needed.

Shaking his head in amazement at the fact that the Pickens physician delivered 3,600 babies in homes up and down the hollers without ever losing a mother, Doc recalled the 100th birthday of Dr. Cunningham when the oldest baby he delivered now 66 years old celebrated along with the youngest baby now 6 years old.

SEVEN NATURAL WONDERS
OF UPSHUR COUNTY

Dr. Harold Almond and Lois, his wife of fifty-one years, supported 4-H with the spirit of the four H's: HEAD, HEART, HANDS, and HEALTH. For years the Upshurite 4-H Club met in the living room of their home. 4-H'ers learned public speaking by giving talks and demonstrations. On the occasion of Dad's 80th birthday he appeared on the TLC TV program and reminisced about the time he had convinced me, his shy teenaged son, to speak of the Seven Natural Wonders of Upshur County. The Upshurite 4-H Club then conducted tours to the seven sights. Local newspapers followed the evolving and ever expanding story.

1—Pringle Tree: This 3rd generation sycamore is hollow in its old age. It is surrounded by a lovely park suitable for picnics.

Lois' sorority Alpha Gamma Delta decided to see how many women could fit in the tree. They squeezed 23 inside and others up on the limbs. A picture taken went around the world on the AP wire service. The picture remains displayed in the Alumni House.

2—Spruce Falls: These are the tallest falls in Upshur County at 50 feet. The stream begins at Light Chapel and flows down to Stone Coal Lake. The falls are just after the stream flows under the Brushy Fork/Glady Fork Road.

3—Split Rock: This sandstone rock formation is 60 feet high by 80-90 feet long with an 18 inch to 30 inch split down the middle. Cutright's History of Upshur County records the fact that when trees grew on top, the ice that formed in the winter would remain all summer.

Once an overweight man got caught in the split and

could not get out. He called for help. Fortunately a Methodist Circuit Rider preacher came along. He pushed and pulled at the man but could not dislodge him. Finally after deliberating for a while he asked him how much he had given to the church in the last year. Well the man had not paid his tithes and offerings. He felt so small that he wiggled right out.

4—Hosaflook Cave: The largest sandstone cave in Upshur County is near the former Hosaflook school about a country mile from the junction of the Selbyville and Alexander roads. The cave is 18 feet high, 50-60 feet across, and 80 feet deep.

When the Hosaflooks owned it the cave was called Hunt's cave. When the Hunts owned it the cave was called Hosaflook's cave. The Woodys currently own it.

5—Upshur Mountain: At 3050 feet, this is the highest peak in Upshur County. It is found south of Hemlock near High Germany.

The 4-H club made signs which were nailed to a tree on top pointing to other high peaks in the world including Mt Fuji, Japan at 12,000 feet, Mt. McKinley, USA at 20,000 feet, and Mt. Everest, Nepal at 29,000 feet.

6—Wagon Wheel Cave: Off of Selbyville road, an oak tree bent across the road when it was young and stood at only five feet. If one takes rock from the floor and scratches it on the ceiling, the ceiling then "effervesces" for several minutes. The unknown cause of this reaction has puzzled many.

Moonshine operations ran out of there in the past. The axle hole made a natural chimney, and the overhanging wheel portion afforded protection from the rain.

7—Natural Bridge at Carter: This two-car bridge, formed of a rock base, can be found one mile from

Chapel.

Many have wryly observed that the State Road Commission saved money on this bridge. The bridge has a four-foot width over the stream meandering through a meadow. It's a lovely place with wild flowers and blackberries.

SHAMOGA OIL

Remedies change. Dr. James Cunningham injected Shamoga Oil to treat the only patient with leprosy ever treated in West Virginia, but Dr. Harold Almond did not have any idea what it did or why a physician would prescribe it. But the three-part adage Doc came back to multiple times on the TLC TV program holds true:

1. Acquire vast sums of knowledge
2. Have keen powers of observation
3. Arrive at some logical conclusion

Doc told the story of his only encounter with leprosy. While Doc was studying at Northwestern University a patient presented symptoms which stumped faculty, so they arranged a clinical pathophysiology conference. Because he had heard of leprosy from his grandmother's reading of the Bible and because he'd read about it hoping to see a case someday, Doc felt sure he knew the diagnosis. When the numbness of the hand was described as a symptom and the flat nose was apparent, Doc felt more encouraged that he was knew the answer. This time, students from Z to A were asked what the diagnosis was. Doc was next to last. He boldly declared that it was Hanson's Disease, a.k.a. leprosy.

"One of you is right," the professor declared and asked Doc to stand. Yes, he was proud and happy.

However, making the diagnosis is only half the doctor's task. Coming up with ways to relieve suffering is the rest. Dr. Cunningham managed to do that with a mysterious potion. But still the question remains: what exactly is Shamoga Oil? For the answer, see page 131.

SWISS CHEESE

On Dr. Harold Almond's last visit to Pickens in 1998 on the occasion of the Maple Syrup Festival, he sat as he customarily would in Dr. James Cunningham's office greeting folks and telling stories. His old friend John Betler came to visit. Upon greeting each other, John said through tears, "I've lost my wife." Doc reached out and hugged him with tears in his own eyes replying, "I've lost mine too."

The friends began talking about "the old times." John Betler recalled that in 1915, Dr. Cunningham went riding by on horseback past his family's farm on the road from Helvetia to Pickens. Inquiringly he asked John's father, "Do you use lime around here?"

"No," young Betler replied.

"You're wrong not to. Your cows will give better milk and you'll have better cheese. Here is $5.00. Get up to WVU agricultural school. You'll be glad you did," Dr. Cunningham advised. The good doctor, always interested in education, knew that the land grant college would teach proper use of lime and other minerals for scientific farming.

So young Betler did as the good doctor prescribed. He took the train down the Buckhannon River from Pickens and then on to Morgantown. On the way back he stopped to pick up eighteen tons of dolomite lime which has both lime and magnesium in it.

From that day on the local farmers spread lime, resulting in beautiful green fields. And their Swiss cheese tastes the best from this Little Switzerland of America.

COURAGEOUS, COMPASSIONATE, AND CREATIVE PRACTICE OF MEDICINE

A MIGHTY BIG PERSON

Occasions of being present at the moment of death have a certain mystery. The local Civil War hero, General Stonewall Jackson, whose boyhood home is in the adjoining county to Upshur, died with his wife and child present. He is reported to have said, "Let us cross the river and go into the trees" at the moment of his death.

Doc recalled his uncle-in-law Paul Barnes' death. The day began as usual with breakfast and taking the children to school. Uncle Paul came to the door asking to go to the hospital. In those days a doctor could hospitalize with little reason, so Doc said okay without inquiring what may be wrong. In any event, no chief complaint was offered.

Uncle Paul picked up his suitcase and walked to the jeep. He climbed up and in without discernible difficulty. Driving past his sister's home he waved good-bye to her. Doc did not recall any further words but he noticed Uncle Paul leaning against the Jeep door as they braked for the stoplight by the courthouse. Checking for a pulse and finding none, Doc drove on to the ER where he found neither breath nor heart sounds.

Greenbrier recalled that as he played during recess at Academy School with his fifth grade friends, a large sixteen-wheel truck passed by with a big van labeled Casket Company. He made the offhanded remark, "There goes a mighty big person." After school he heard from his mother that Uncle Paul had died that day. She characterized him as a mighty big person.

ALL CLOGGING ASIDE

Accidents happen.

Out at Excelsior just as the strawberries bloomed, a little six-year old girl fractured her fibula. Her family was poor, and there was simply no way they could afford the necessary cast or crutches.

Doc had some extra plaster of Paris which he used for casting. Recalling that Dr. James Cunningham of Pickens made his own prostheses including an apple wood peg leg, Doc decided to make a crutch for his little patient. He cut a hickory limb and split it halfway down. After measuring for the height up to the armpit, he made a comfortable rest and covered it with a cushion. Off a chair he took a rubber tip and covered the end.

Now his little patient could mend and yet remain mobile.

What surprised Doc was how mobile she became. She got along better than anyone he'd ever known. In fact, she could even run with her crutch. Not one to leave a lighted candle under a bushel, Doc encouraged her to enter the Strawberry Festival Grand Feature Parade where she became the hit of the show. She drew more applause than even the clogging Congressman and future governor Bob Wise.

AM I GOING TO DIE?

A farmer and his son fished down the Buckhannon River from Alton on Labor Day of 1957. Fish were biting. Then a mile below Alton, the son crossed a meadow heading toward a new pool to fish when a 20-inch copperhead bit him hard on the Achilles Heel. His father rushed to his aid stoning the snake and applying a tourniquet near the knee, cutting two x's over the fang wounds and sucking out venom.

"Am I going to die, Daddy?" the son asked repeatedly. Keeping calm and reassuring his son, the two made their way back up the railroad track to their truck and headed for Buckhannon. Stopping at a phone in Evergreen, the farmer called ahead to Doc who told them to meet him at St. Joseph's Hospital.

At least four times a summer snakebite victims presented to St. Joseph's ER, usually with good results. The son remained anxious as Doc and Sister Agastine treated him. He asked again, "Am I going to die, Doc?" Fortunately the bite was far from the heart and the farmer had applied good first aid. Antivenin treatment and continually sucking out venom every fifteen minutes for four hours worked. The boy lived.

In his telling of the story, Doc recalled that the son did not grow an inch nor gain a pound for the next fifteen months. Then he shot up to six feet, eight inches tall and two-hundred fifty pounds. He went on to West Virginia University and then into the Navy where he completed dentistry education. He has a wonderful career and now is a professor of dentistry.

Doc was so impressed with the first aid the farmer

rendered to his son that he determined that from 1957 on all boys in Upshur County should be granted an opportunity to learn similar survival skills. Doc bought Boy Scout Merit Badge books for all badges required for the Eagle Rank, Boy Scouts' highest honor, and presented them to the Charles Gibson library. Then he contacted professionals proficient in each merit badge skill, asking them to teach boys who wanted to learn.

Doc continued teaching the First Aid Merit Badge to many boys throughout the rest of his life. Greenbrier, his son, learned first aid from Doc and completed all other merit badges, joining the rank of Eagle Scout with his father's encouragement.

CLEAR TO FIREWALL

Delivering babies has always been a happy part of practicing medicine, Harold Almond, MD laughed.

Doc participated in the miracle of welcoming new life 3,600 times.

Triplets are rare, but Doc got his chance to deliver a set during his internship in Chicago with a clinic patient who had had no pre-natal care. Mother and babies did well with Doc's help.

While in Japan flying to a hospital in an Air Force cargo plane he delivered a baby whose father was a military policeman. The pilot did everything he could to arrive at the hospital before the baby arrived in the world, but the baby was coming quickly. When ordered to hurry he declared, "I've got it clear to the firewall!" When he heard the baby's cry he slowed the plane and Doc felt that he, mother, and baby were floating.

Twins are rare, too—one set of twins for every eighty-eight single deliveries. Doc experienced the adventure of a lifetime when a couple from Gaines who already had six children delivered twins. Wow! But in twelve months the mother delivered another set of twins. Double Wow! But wait, in twelve more months this dear lady delivered another set of twins. Triple Wow! Then she became pregnant again but this time she had a single baby. And Doc was there for them all!

DELIVERING A CHILD—IT TAKES A VILLAGE

Thanksgiving 1950 is one for the history books. Snow, snow, and more snow, fifty inches deep.

Doc and Lois expected some excitement that Thanksgiving as their third child's due date matched the holiday. But now the falling snow and the promise of more required well thought-out strategy. Grace from the office planned to stay with little Greenbrier and K. Ole' Friendly Bud Bennett, Buckhannon's fire chief, bulldozed the road up the hill and around the City Park to the Almond residence.

The latest Almond hurried her entrance into the cold, cold world after a house call. Because the elderly Clark couple up the street needed medicine, Lois delivered it by trudging through the deep snow up the hill to their farm house and back down again. And then came the baby.

What a grand entrance to the village of Buckhannon for Mary Anne Almond, November 28, 1950.

HAROLD D. ALMOND HEALTH CENTER

"Making the Best Better" was doubtless more than a 4-H motto for Doc; he lived it daily. The naming of the Upshur County Youth Camp nursing quarters / health center after Doc testifies to the difference he made. The week after his beloved Lois passed on to Glory, he drove to Selbyville to see the 4-H youth in action.

He proudly displayed a postcard picture of the camp taken by Howard Hiner 25 years earlier. The photo was snapped at exactly 11:10 am to get the precise lighting the photographer desired. Doc laughed as he recalled that the fall leaves were off the trees at Selbyville, but a flash of color was needed in the pose. Always creative problem-solvers, Lois and he had scotch-taped red leaves onto a branch that was "growing" near the Glenn Ford Water Fountain. The Arlie Smith Assembly Hall gleams in the background, and to the side the Newton Anderson Dining Hall welcomes all for a good meal.

Doc recalled Dr. Bill Carper receiving a copy of the postcard, mailed to his retirement home in Florida. He showed it around, so enthralled by the beauty that he also sent a $1,000 check for camp improvements.

Dr. Bill Hallam surveyed the new Council Circle, then Doc and Raymond Lockwood poured the concrete for the risers. Oh how dismayed Doc was when he realized that he had poured one set of risers nine inches higher than the rest. Again his longtime life partner, Lois, came to the rescue by graciously pointing out that the Big Feet Tribe needed the extra leg room.

I AM WILLING

"Dad, how do you explain the success of your medical practice?" I asked my father, Dr. Harold Almond, as I introduced him as a special guest on the Tender Loving Care TV program. Indeed he was back "for the umpteenth time" to tell more of his stories.

Without so much as catching his breath Doc replied, "I always tried to exceed my patient's expectation!"

"Dad, that is a recipe for burnout. No one can expect to exceed another person's expectations 100% of the time," I cautioned.

But Doc stuck to his guns, relaying a promise he made to God at age ten. His infant brother had developed erysiphylis and died after three weeks. The doctors had no antibiotics and were treating his brother with only witch hazel. The young Harold vowed, "If God gave me a chance to practice medicine, then I'd give my best."

From that promise of a youth sprang forth an abundant life of practicing the healing profession. There were many steps forward as well as some steps backward. Doc explained how when the Great Depression came, his family lived for six months off the $50.00 he had earned as a golf caddy. Then as the Depression continued he worked hard for seven years helping to build the Appalachian Trail in New England and the Long Trail in Vermont. During fire season he would sit atop fire towers monitoring the area for forest fires. He fondly remembered, "I could not come down unless it rained. So I determined to read the 100 greatest books ever written while atop my perch. I gained a college education from reading."

Finally when he could come to West Virginia Wesleyan College upon the recommendation of his New Jersey Methodist minister, he worked as a waiter and as a lab assistant. Medical school remained a goal but then the attack on Pearl Harbor with World War II modified his plans. "Actually, I could not afford Northwestern University in Chicago but the Army Air Force paid the way." After eight years of service, he finally arrived back in Buckhannon, West Virginia with Lois, his college sweetheart, and their growing family.

"The early months of practice proved slow and lean with many patients not wanting to trust the new young redheaded physician. Then in February 1950 we had a flu epidemic, the worst I've ever seen," Doc quipped. "I've been busy ever since," he added.

Doc summed up his reflection with a most revealing comment: "From the moment that I told God 'I am willing,' all I ever wanted to do was practice medicine, and I got my chance!"

LIVING WATER

"Jesus answered . . . thou wouldest have asked of him, and he would have given thee living water," concluded the Biblical theme of the night from the 4th chapter of the Gospel of John. Each show of the Tender, Loving Care TV program consists of an examination of the interface between Christianity and medicine. Dr. Harold Almond always honored that principle and he always embellished it with a most creative and original touch. The program had become the most-watched half hour on channel 3, Buckhannon's local access channel, due in large part to Doc's stories.

The Buckhannon Rotary Club had asked Doc to share the importance of a clean water supply to the growth of the community. He left the Rotarians scratching their heads, pondering how to carry out his proposals. Doc began with how important pure water is to life itself. He told the civic group, and now was repeating the talk for the entire viewing audience, how nearly 50 years earlier he had treated seven Typhoid Fever patients in the area whose illnesses were the result of contaminated water.

Dr. Harold Almond made many country house calls, often putting 60,000 miles or more each year on his Jeep. He always thought about ways to improve the watershed of the Buckhannon River. This night he shared his professional opinion and personal belief that Upshur County needed a dam above Helvetia "about thirty feet high and about one hundred feet long" to ensure a clean water supply.

Buckhannon's water system began as a private enterprise in 1902 when a water plant operated near the Poe Bridge. Basically it was a simple operation of pumping water out of the Buckhannon River, filtering out the Giardia, and adding Chlorine—one part per million. Then the water pump filled a 250,000 gallon wooden tank up on the water tank hill. A senior Rotarian, Charlie Wereley, added to the history by recalling the rupture of the tank in 1927. So much water poured down the hill that a house on Kanawha Street was washed off its foundation and into the middle of the street.

Dr. Harold Almond began his practice in Buckhannon in 1949, returning after eight years of military service in the Army Air Force during and after WW II. He saluted the Pallotine Order of Sisters who came to town as a missionary order from Germany and opened the first St. Joseph's Hospital. The old Barlow House was the mansion on the hill at the end of Main Street. How grand it was to practice in a 50-bed hospital that had round tower rooms for patients. Doc recalled that a 25,000 gallon wooden water tank was needed for water pressure and for fire protection. In 1964 the community and the Sisters joined in building a new hospital including a joint effort of constructing a 600,000 gallon tank.

After describing each and every one of the seventeen water tanks in the county, Doc paid respect to "living water" noting he had made house calls in all three of the Upshur County homes where artesian wells bubble up spontaneously. "I just marvel that God can supply all this water."

MIRACLES AND HEALING

Sunday dinner after church service proved a great time to work up the next TLC TV program. On this occasion we had a new preacher whose sermon series was on Jesus, the Great Physician. Doc said he had stories of compassion which we could match with the Scriptures. "What we have today that Jesus did not have is follow-through.We do not have any record of what happened to the lepers Jesus healed. And what happened to Lazarus after he was raised from the dead?"

Lights, camera, action.

The following Tuesday at 7:00 pm Dr. Harold Almond and I prayed together as was our custom just before we went on the air. A profound thought came to mind: my rare privilege has been to know this man as Dad, as mentoring doctor, as co-disciple of Jesus as Lord and Savior.

"And there came a leper to him, beseeching him, and kneeling down to him, and saying unto him, 'If thou wilt, thou canst make me clean.' And Jesus, moved with compassion, put forth his hand, and touched him, and saith unto him, 'I will; be thou clean.'"

Doc expounded, "What Mark has recorded about Dr. Jesus' care of the leper is what Dr. Cunningham did for the leper of Pickens, West Virginia. Both showed compassion. Both touched the lepers." We discussed further how now we have leprosariums in the United States in Louisiana and Hawaii. Furthermore we have "miracle drugs" including the triple therapy antibiotics for leprosy so the patients are not infectious. With follow-through we can provide good nutrition, good hygiene, and good medication.

Doc summarized, "We have miracle drugs but not miracle doctors." That may be so, but doctors with the compassion of Dr. Harold Almond come awfully close.

MOST CHOSEN PROFESSION

Describing to his granddaughter, Maria, the intimate relationship a physician has with his patients, Harold D. Almond, MD characterized medicine as the most chosen profession by God, even more than ministry. He spoke of the first Doctor's Day in Georgia, March 30, 1935, when Eudora Almond (not a known relationship with the West Virginia Almonds) lifted up her husband, Charles Almond, MD and all doctors.

Doc honored Dr. James Cunningham and earlier doctors by saying, "Those were a lot stronger doctors." He was impressed with the ability of Dr. Cunningham to deliver 3,600 babies in the home and not lose a single mother. His "Dr. Stork" role at eight hours per delivery for 3,600 babies had occupied ten years of his more than sixty-five years of practicing medicine.

And why practice in a small town? Doc enjoyed the healing relationship found both in the intimacy of sharing in a patient's moments of greatest suffering and distress, and also in the witnessing of growth throughout the years. "Healing the sick is also announcing the Kingdom of God near to us," Doc maintained.

Greenbrier remembered answering a telephone call in mid-afternoon when Dad was in the garden. "Yes, he is here but he is working in the garden; may I take a message?" Hearing from the voice on the line that this was an emergency, he recognized that the doctor was needed. Dad trudged up the hill looking like the raspberry-weeding was invigorating. But the energy was draining out of him the further he walked from the berries. Doc would say, "I'll be right out." He always went and did the best he could.

MOST LAZY

Doc was self-motivated all his life. Before multi-tasking was popular he exemplified it, so his disdain for anyone who looked for ways not to work can be understood. Doc shook his head as if he could not believe this happened when he told the story of the man who was putting in a "very small garden" with a six-inch diameter tree in the middle of the garden plot.

Apparently the saw was dull and slow to cut, so the man decided to climb up in the tree and sway it back and forth. He leaned one way a bit too much and the tree crashed down with him up in it. He sustained two Colle's fractures, one of each wrist. Doc told him he would not be able to work for at least six weeks. In fact he would need to be shaved and fed.

"Oh Doc, I want a slip telling my employer I cannot work for six <u>months</u>. I'll probably never work again," the lazy man proclaimed.

MT. FUJI TRAUMA

Emotional trauma can be repressed, almost for a lifetime.

When Harold Almond, MD described to his psychiatrist son, Greenbrier, his Air Force experience in Japan, he did so within a month of his death. Doc served as one of two physicians assigned with General Douglas MacArthur to the military occupation of Japan. He left his pregnant wife, Lois, and young son, Greenbrier, in Nebraska at the Kearney Air Force Base. World War II had already taken a toll on the Almond family; his brother Ralph, an Air Force pilot, had been shot down and lost in the Pacific Ocean.

"Captain Almond, we need you to take a crew of men to inspect the plane crash on Mt. Fuji. You know it is 10,000 feet up the 12,000 foot peak, so be prepared."

In fact, Doc had spent years preparing. He had a vigorous Boy Scout heritage and years of experience hiking and camping the top two-thirds of the Appalachian Trail. But then again, how can one ever truly be prepared for a plane crash?

The air was thin and breathing was painful. The cold, snowy wind whipped around his body. The task of recovering body parts strewn across the steep mountain terrain boggled his mind. The reminder that this world war that had forever changed his family and himself was still not over saddened his soul.

This is a story Doc almost did not want to tell.

NAVEL OF A GOOD NURSE

Doc influenced many lives. Ever observant, he looked for certain traits in children. Did they like puzzles? Were they curious? Did they show common sense? Whenever he saw a winning combination he'd look at the child in all seriousness and say in a slightly lowered voice, "You'd make a good nurse."

Only years later did evidence prove that Doc's message and encouragement had impact. Young girls' lives were changed for the better and health care improved for a whole generation of patients.

These were good nurses. Public health department heads. Nursing professors. Surgical nurses. Medical nurses. Missionary nurses. All shapes and varieties.

But the strangest compliment, indicating his positive influence, came when a very capable nurse approached Doc to say, "I am a nurse today because when I was just a girl you made a house call to see me with my bellyache. You told me, after an exam of my abdomen, that I had the navel of a nurse!"

Doc just shook his head back and forth and smiled.

OFF LABEL

Miracle drugs include not only antibiotics but also anti-headache preparations. Doc marveled about Imitrex. The medication is self-injected by the patient experiencing a migraine and works wonders for many patients suffering the often debilitating pain. Doc recalled the early days of his practice when he used glass syringes that needed autoclaved for sterilization after every use. The needles were also used again and again. Indeed he would sharpen his needles every month with a whetstone. He recalled that Louis Carroll suffered from migraine headaches. Unbeknownst to many readers, his book *Alice's Adventures in Wonderland* describes the clinical syndrome in creative language. Even Queen Victoria loved the book. She told Carroll to give her a copy of any other book he might write as she'd love to read it as well. By profession Louis Carroll was a mathematics professor. His next book was on differential calculus. The queen received her copy as requested but doubtless she never read it.

Terramycin proved a miracle drug twice, Doc recalled. He had a fourteen-year old girl come in with a surgical belly. Dr. Basil Page and he operated only to find extensive pus and flaming pelvic inflammatory disease. Doc began Terramycin, a new medication at the time. For three days he had to keep warning the parents that their little girl might not make it. But by the third day, Doc realized she would live, so he told the parents she was hanging in there. Again when she was eighteen she returned with PID and again responded well to Terramycin. Finally she became pregnant and Doc followed her pregnancy fearing complications from adhesions as delivery approached. However, at eight and a half months gestation she delivered a healthy baby.

SPIDER BITES

A man and his wife were driving toward Buckhannon from Weston. Suddenly she screamed out in agony. As she fainted away she told her husband she had batted a spider off her arm. He flagged down a policeman who directed them to Dr. Harold Almond's office.

Doc answered the summons to their car. The woman appeared dead. He spotted a dreaded black widow spider on the floor. "Hurry," he yelled to his nurse, "get the calcium gluconate and start an IV." In a few minutes the woman began to complain "ouch, ouch, it hurts!" rubbing her spider bitten arm. Her alertness and awareness of the pain were welcome signs that she would be okay.

When asked how he knew calcium gluconate was the antidote for black widow spider bites, the good doctor modestly declared, "Some things you always remember."

TEACHERS

Tender, loving care definitely applied to teaching, according to Dr. Harold Almond. To make his point he told stories of three teachers he greatly admired.

Mini Merle graduated from West Virginia Wesleyan College in the early part of the 20th century. She had a truly amazing world-wide teaching career, being a professor at the University of Paris, Temple University, University of Virginia, University of Alaska, and Salem College in West Virginia.

It was at Salem that she taught young Cecil Underwood who later served West Virginia as the state's youngest Governor and then as the state's oldest Governor.

Doc recalled that Mini Merle retired to Buckhannon and lived near the college. She was quite a character, bold and outspoken. He admired those traits in her. After settling in, she realized her teaching career was incomplete as she had never taught in a one-room school house. She presented her teaching credentials to the Upshur County Board of Education asking to teach in a one-room school. There was an opening at Hemlock, and she got the nod.

While she was an excellent teacher, her driving left something to be desired. She would drive right down the middle of the road, Doc remembered. The road to Hemlock was gravel base from upper Queens up the steep mountain and along the five-mile ridge road. It was on the hill that Mini Merle spun her tires and threw rocks out which hit her car. This frustrated the old school ma'am greatly, but she quickly solved her problem. She called up

Governor Underwood: "Cecil, this is your teacher Mini Merle and I'm ordering you to pave that road up the hill out of Queens."

The next day the State Road Commission was out paving.

Doc held the highest esteem for Helen Reger. She taught school for years with a normal degree, an abbreviated course of study that allowed new high school graduates to teach. In 1955 she pioneered the first public kindergarten in West Virginia beginning in an old house on Victoria Street in Buckhannon. Ruthie, the third daughter of Harold and Lois Almond, was the very first graduate.

Mrs. Reger's reputation as a fine kindergarten teacher spread far and wide. University and college students sought experience teaching practicums under her tutelage.

She realized something was missing in her résumé: she did not have any graduate degree in kindergarten teaching. Seeking to remedy the problem, she applied to Marshall University. They looked over her background and told her she would have to apply to graduate school and attend classes.

In her tender loving care manner Helen Reger informed Marshall University that she was already teaching their graduate students. Recognizing her point, the University promptly gave her an oral exam which she passed. They then granted her a degree to make her legal.

Melvin Claudius Daniel always had a warm spot in

Doc's heart. He grew up "on the hill" where he was in and out of the Almond family home daily. This evening Doc lifted "Danny" up as one of the most outstanding teachers West Virginia Wesleyan College ever graduated. Year after year he was recognized as the Outstanding Teacher in Wood County. In fact he has received the Alumni Award from Wesleyan, too.

Always focusing on the unusual aspects of an individual, Doc appeared most pleased that Melvin Daniel had been honored to be pictured on the cover of the C & P Telephone Book.

THE CRADLE

Doc loved obstetrics. At least he loved the delivery of healthy children. The dark side of "OB" including rape and incest "really made me sick!" He had treated many young girls coming in with infections after back-alley abortions, especially when serving at St. Luke's Hospital in Chicago. Yes, those were dangerous days for the healthy mother electing abortion, no matter how the pregnancy began.

A sad case in Upshur County weighed on Doc's soul. There was a 33-year-old retarded lady who presented to his office not even realizing she was pregnant. He could feel the baby kicking. The blood pressure was high. She had 4+ albumin in the urine. Her risk of seizing and dying was real. Dr. Huffman consulted and agreed that a referral to West Virginia University Hospital would be best. Indeed, a cesarean saved the mother and the child who was adopted out.

Doc fondly recalled "The Cradle," a home for unwed mothers in Chicago. There pregnant single women lived in a safe environment, had good prenatal care, attended church, and in due time delivered their babies who were then adopted out. Then the women could continue their education and their babies could be given the gift of life.

THE WISDOM OF SOLOMON

Dr. Almond's cousin Shirley came to Buckhannon from W.V.U. School of Nursing for spring break of her sophomore year. Doc was convinced she needed some clinical experience with a country doctor. They spent the week making house calls, visiting 100-year-old Dr. James Cunningham, and performing emergency surgery at St. Joseph's Hospital.

Of course, Shirley may not have been prepared in her wildest dreams for some of what she experienced. Late one night the telephone rang. "Would you come to treat our little girl? She is so sick."

"Yes, my cousin and I are on our way," Doc promised. On the way down he asked Shirley to be particularly observant. The home they were visiting was unusual—the man had two wives. Shirley was to figure out which of the two wives was the mother of the child!

Doc reminded her of 1 Kings chapter 3 in which two women living in the same household each had a child but then one child died when the mother rolled over on him. In the middle of the night this mother substituted the dead child with the live child sleeping with his mother. In the morning light the second mother discovered the dead child in bed with her and immediately realized it was not her own. It was left to Solomon to determine the true mother. He ordered that a sword cut the live baby in two, declaring that he would give half to one woman and half to the other. In the story, the true mother was overcome with love for her child and begged for Solomon to give the whole live baby to the other woman rather than see it die. At that point Solomon in God's wisdom gave the baby to the woman begging to keep the baby alive, the true mother.

What did Shirley decide???

TOUCHING THE HEM OF THE GARMENT

Bleeding is a medical emergency. Dr. Harold Almond kept up-to-date on all such life and death ailments. He kept a detective's eye out for poisoning, another medical emergency. Respiratory distress and emergent care for shortness of breath also remained high on his therapeutic acumen. He always remembered his brother's death as a child from pneumonia. As a doctor he welcomed the opportunity to help the truly, desperately ill. He reasoned that seeing patients without appointment in his office allowed him to render more acute sickness care. "If I worked by appointment I would only see my patient two weeks after he was well or hear about his death from family members."

The Tender Loving Care TV program afforded Doc an opportunity to explore the interface between Medicine and Christianity. He conducted his guest appearances like he did the kitchen fireside chats he and his "sugar plum" Lois would hold forth in their home. On this particular evening the physiology and biochemistry of blood was on his mind. The Gospel of Mark records a story of the woman who had an issue of blood for twelve years. Doc was fascinated by her history. She had suffered many things of many physicians. On the day of her healing she determined to press through the crowd and touch Jesus' clothes. She believed this would lead to her healing. "No appointment necessary," Doc wryly observed.

Dr. Harold Almond recalled how he had been able to help patients with blood dyscrasia. Working with Dr. Freeman, a local pediatrician, they had treated a baby with erythroblastosis by taking two ounces of cord blood out of the baby and putting two ounces of healthy blood in. Over several hours they exchanged the baby's blood, and the baby lived. Then there was the school teacher who lived at Czar near Helvetia. She had a very high titer of Rh negative blood. This would save the lives of babies if transfused. She gave a pint of blood every three months for three or four years. Doc helped her connect with a hospital in New Jersey which would receive her donation, always the good doctor, always going the extra mile to help the sick.

TREATING WHAT AILS

Going from 38 specific medications at the beginning of Dr. Harold Almond's medical career to 3000 specific medications available to treat disease by the close truly made for the golden era of medicine. Doc prepared several TLC programs in cooperation with local pharmacists highlighting the marvelous scientific progress he had witnessed.

Laughing, he told of his first "A" in medical school at Northwestern University. It was almost his first "F." The Infectious Disease professor, Dr. Sutton, was lecturing on a new antibiotic, Sulfa. Doc sat up front since his name began with "A." He listened attentively as the professor described one form of Sulfa that crystallized in the kidney 62% of the time, causing serious side effects. He pointed out a high risk for rash, too. But then he said a newer form of Sulfa only crystallized 33% of the time. This was still unacceptable but did save lives. Now the latest Sulfa only crystallized in the kidneys 18% of the time, better but still not good enough.

Dr. Hyma's lecture at West Virginia Wesleyan College on the solubility of salts came to Doc's mind as he sat in the medical school classroom. To focus his thinking, Doc closed his eyes. He could see the chalkboard diagramming Dr. Hyma had provided. He recalled the central point: each salt is soluble in its own right regardless of the other salts in the solution.

Suddenly the Infectious Disease professor was yelling at the young red-headed student in the first row with closed eyes. "There will be no sleeping in my class!" he thundered. "What is your explanation? It better be good or an "F" to you."

Young Harold slowly began to speak. "No, I'm not sleeping. I closed my eyes so I could think better. My Physical Chemistry professor at West Virginia Wesleyan College taught us that salts like the Sulfa antibiotic can ALL dissolve in solution. What you need to do, Doctor, is to use lower doses of each Sulfa creating a Triple-Sulfa solution. Then all the patients will get a higher concentration of antibiotic and increase their chances of benefiting with no crystallizing in the kidneys."

"That's the most stupid thing I've ever heard!" the professor declared. However, he did go back to talk to one of the chemistry professors who lived next door to him in Evanston, Illinois.

The next class, he had the young student stand. He said that he owed an apology to Harold Almond. Furthermore, he told the class, "I'm giving my first "A" in this class." He then enthusiastically announced that Cook County Hospital was using Triple-Sulfa antibiotic therapy right then, and lives were being saved.

TWO QUESTIONS

Lois and Harold Almond, being children of the Great Depression, sought a simple life unencumbered with debt. In the early years of his medical practice they lived in an inexpensive rental house along Jaw Bone Creek where spring floods could be expected. The family grew so they moved into a garage apartment on land purchased overlooking Buckhannon and out of the flood plain. Finally, with four children crowding their humble quarters, the family home construction phase began on their land. For Ruthie Almond, the youngest child at that time, her first word was certainly telling: "bulldozer."

After moving into a house with a grand view, a cozy fireplace and plenty of living space, the time for new furniture was at hand. Lois and Doc met with master carpenter Rudolph Zumbach of Helvetia, West Virginia. He listened to their request for a dining room table where no one would ever bump their feet or shins and if children crawled all over it, the table would never tip. Doc had a special request for stools instead of chairs.

Two questions were asked of the couple:

"What wood?" and

"How high for the tabletop?"

Soon the finest maple table in all of Buckhannon graced the Almond family home. And fifty years later the table and stools are as good as the day they were made.

WHO GOES FIRST?

Dr. Harold Almond had many recurring themes, or as his daughter K characterizes it, he had many signatures. Each of these themes is the mark of the person he became in his nearly 45 years as a country doctor. On the occasion of this Tender, Loving Care TV program he spoke of courage and daring in solving medical mysteries. For a man who read every Earl Stanley Gardner "Perry Mason" book ever published, mostly at night while waiting to deliver a baby, this was a well-considered topic.

"Someone has to take the risk of being the first human being guinea pig!" Doc explained. "Often a doctor is the one who allows a new procedure to be tried on his body. This is at great risk to the doctor's health; he may die."

"Take Pellagra," Doc instructed. Pellagra is a disease causing gastrointestinal, neurologic, mental, cutaneous, and mucosal symptoms. "In the southern end of the county I had to treat a mountaineer's dog before he'd let me treat his wife. Thanks to Dr. Goldberger who in 1906 discovered the root cause of this nutritional disorder, I was on solid scientific ground. In the economic depression sweeping the country in the early 1900s, prisons, mental institutions, poor farms, and old folks homes were cutting back what they fed their charges. Health and well-being deteriorated in the institutionalized but not the employees. It was a mystery.

"Young Dr. Goldberger took the train down to Alabama from New York City, determined to solve the health crisis. He had to rule out bacterial disease, so he made a concoction of diseased skin, urine, and feces from his patients and swallowed it. No disease resulted, so the cause was not infectious. Yet many continued developing the "4 D's" of dermatitis, dementia, diarrhea, and death. This led the good doctor to consider nutritional causes. He ordered an improved diet of green leafy vegetables containing nicotinic acid. His patients recovered."

Dr. Harold Almond laughed as he continued to describe medical mysteries solved by a doctor who would go first. In Denmark, scabies was a problem. By chance a pharmaceutical house discovered that disulfiram killed the parasite. "The doctor in charge took the cure first. Lo and behold" Doc declared, "it worked and with no side effects. At least not until the doctor brought his sack lunch which included a beer. Just as he was finishing lunch his pulse became very rapid, his face flushed red as a beet, and his blood pressure rose to stroke range."

"The beer was being converted to acetaldehyde because of the disulfiram. While the doctor could have died, he did not. Instead he discovered 'the pill of last chance' for alcoholics." When a patient suffering from alcoholism takes disulfiram everyday he and his family have assurance that he will not drink because of the risk of deathly sickness.

"Dr. Forman received the Nobel Prize in Medicine in 1956 for solving the next medical mystery," Doc reported. The story began in 1929 when he worked in a Red Cross hospital in Berlin, Germany. No one believed the heart could be catheterized. "Common wisdom, indeed, indicated the heart to be supersensitive to any foreign body. Instant death would result if any foreign body touched the life pump.

"Well the good doctor believed otherwise. He sugared up to the surgical nurse," Dr. Almond declared, "so she gave him supplies including rubber urinary catheters. Most amazingly, the young doctor catheterized himself.

He then repeated the experiment nine times with x-ray evidence.

"Now we have the medical specialty of invasive cardiology because Dr. Forman would go first!"

Finally, that night on the Tender, Loving Care TV program, Dr. Harold Almond told the wonderful story of Walter Reed, MD and colleagues who risked their lives to discover the cause of Yellow Fever. The USA was fighting Spain in 1898. In Cuba more troops died of Yellow Fever than from wounds of battle. The French had been stymied in building the Panama Canal due to Yellow Fever plague. Truly it was a mystery that needed solved.

"The liver of patients with Yellow Fever failed, thus resulting in the yellow skin. With no liver doing its 100 tasks for the body, blood would not clot and death followed. Bad air was blamed. Smoke was thought to get rid of bad air so actually tobacco smoking was encouraged by doctors. In Havana, Cuba, natives reported a mosquito bite was to blame. How to prove it?"

Doc ardently praised a medical student who volunteered to sleep in the unclean beds of four patients who died of Yellow Fever. He did not get sick, lessening the odds that a simple contagion was to blame.

"Dr. Laser agreed to let the mosquitoes bite him. Unfortunately he developed Yellow Fever and died. We owe him a great debt," Doc declared. Dr. Walter Reed and other colleagues went on to prove Yellow Fever transmission from the mosquito bite, thus allowing the Americans to win the Spanish-American War, build the Panama Canal, and develop the public health movement.

All because a doctor went first.

After the first printing of this book, I received an email from a reader with an answer to the question posed in the story "Shamoga Oil."

Dear Greenbrier,

On page 94 of your *Tender Loving Care: Stories of a West Virginia Doctor, Volume Two*, you have a story entitled "Shamoga Oil" at the end of which you ask "What exactly is Shamoga Oil?" Well, I believe I can answer that question for you.

Chaulmoogra oil has been used for Hansen's Disease as well as for some other bacterially produced skin lesions. The oil consists of glyceryl esters of chaulmoogric acid and hydnocarpic acids. Other esters of those acids have been used. For all I know, chaulmoogric acid esters are still used in certain instances, although I know it is not the routine therapy for leprosy anymore. *Merck Index* has a little more information on the oil and the acid.

It's hard to believe that Shamoga oil and chaulmoogra oil could be used for the same disease and have names that are so similar, yet not be the same thing. Hence I believe they are the same.

G. Paul Richter

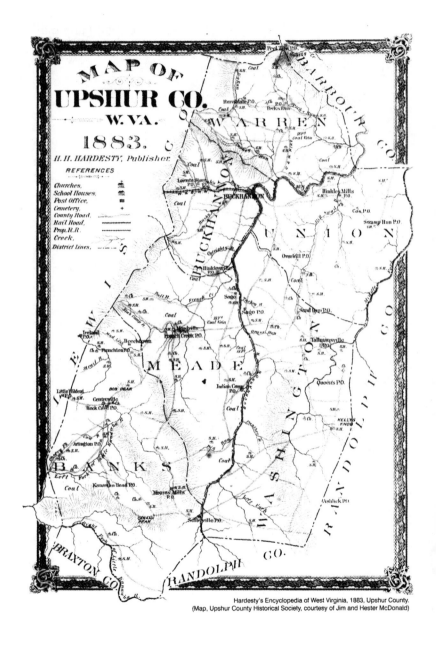

Hardesty's Encyclopedia of West Virginia, 1883, Upshur County.
(Map, Upshur County Historical Society, courtesy of Jim and Hester McDonald)